THE SONG OF THE CARDINAL

THE SONG
OF THE
CARDINAL

Gene Stratton-Porter

———————— • ————————

Amereon House
MATTITUCK, NEW YORK

Library of Congress Catalog Card Number 81-67633
International Standard Book Number 0-89190-945-1

We gratefully acknowledge
the assistance of
The Museum Shop
Indiana State Museum
202 North Alabama
Indianapolis, Indiana 46204

Made and Printed in the United States of America

IN LOVING TRIBUTE
TO THE MEMORY OF MY FATHER
MARK STRATTON

*"For him every work of God manifested a
new and heretofore unappreciated loveliness."*

GENE STRATTON PORTER
1868 - 1924

With the republishing of this book, we welcome the opportunity to introduce a new generation of readers to the enchanting world of Gene Stratton Porter.

To understand Porter's importance as an early twentieth-century writer, it is helpful to know that she was first and foremost a naturalist. Her first published works were charter studies of birds and moths, meticulously recorded and photographed in the great Limberlost Swamp near her home in Geneva, Indiana.

Her novels, for which she is best remembered, were primarily a means to an end. In adopting the fictional form, she hoped to influence a larger audience than could be reached through the traditional nature publications.

Weaving natural lore into plots about simple people, drawn from her own experience, she captivated America with such novels as *Girl of the Limberlost*, *Freckles* and *The Magic Garden*. In doing so, she created a new constituency for conservation of the natural habitat.

In addition to writing prolifically for national magazines, she published twenty-three books during her lifetime. Her immense popularity is reflected by the fact that she was published in seven foreign languages, and was the first American writer to be translated into Arabic. When three of her novels were produced as films, her career took her to Hollywood, where she died in an automobile accident in 1924 at the age of 61.

The product of a unique childhood environment,

Stratton-Porter spent her early years on a remote farm near Wabash, Indiana. Since there was no opportunity for schooling until the family moved into town when Gene was eleven, she learned at the knee of her father. Mark Stratton was an ordained minister, a self-taught naturalist, and a man of broadranging knowledge, who gave his daughter an education that probably could not have been duplicated in any other setting. With the outdoors as her classroom, she became a keen observer of nature, and developed a deep respect for the natural balance of living things.

Later, she was also fortunate in her choice of a husband. In an era that placed suffocating restrictions on the activities of women, Charles Darwin Porter, a prosperous druggist and banker, encouraged his wife to submit her scientific studies for publication, and supported her staunchly throughout her career.

THE SONG OF THE CARDINAL

*"Good cheer! Good cheer!" exulted
the Cardinal*

I

"*Good cheer! Good cheer!*" *exulted the Cardinal*

HE DARTED through the orange orchard searching for slugs for his breakfast, and between whiles he rocked on the branches and rang over his message of encouragement to men. The song of the Cardinal was overflowing with joy, for this was his holiday, his playtime. The southern world was filled with brilliant sunshine, gaudy flowers, an abundance of fruit, myriads of insects, and never a thing to do except to bathe, feast, and be happy. No wonder his song was a prophecy of good cheer for the future, for happiness made up the whole of his past.

The Cardinal was only a yearling, yet his crest

flared high, his beard was crisp and black, and he was a very prodigy in size and colouring. Fathers of his family that had accomplished many migrations appeared small beside him, and coats that had been shed season after season seemed dull compared with his. It was as if a pulsing heart of flame passed by when he came winging through the orchard.

Last season the Cardinal had pipped his shell, away to the north, in that paradise of the birds, the Limberlost. There thousands of acres of black marsh-muck stretch under summers' sun and winters' snows. There are darksome pools of murky water, bits of swale, and high morass. Giants of the forest reach skyward, or, coated with velvet slime, lie decaying in sun-flecked pools, while the underbrush is almost impenetrable.

The swamp resembles a big dining-table for the birds. Wild grape-vines clamber to the tops of the highest trees, spreading umbrella-wise over the branches, and their festooned floating trailers wave as silken fringe in the play of the wind. The birds

4

loll in the shade, peel bark, gather dried curlers for nest material, and feast on the pungent fruit. They chatter in swarms over the wild-cherry trees, and overload their crops with red haws, wild plums, papaws, blackberries and mandrake. The alders around the edge draw flocks in search of berries, and the marsh grasses and weeds are weighted with seed hunters. The muck is alive with worms; and the whole swamp ablaze with flowers, whose colours and perfumes attract myriads of insects and butterflies.

Wild creepers flaunt their red and gold from the treetops, and the bumblebees and humming-birds make common cause in rifling the honey-laden trumpets. The air around the wild-plum and red-haw trees is vibrant with the beating wings of millions of wild bees, and the bee-birds feast to gluttony. The fetid odours of the swamp draw insects in swarms, and fly-catchers tumble and twist in air in pursuit of them.

Every hollow tree homes its colony of bats. Snakes sun on the bushes. The water folk leave

5

trails of shining ripples in their wake as they cross the lagoons. Turtles waddle clumsily from the logs. Frogs take graceful leaps from pool to pool. Everything native to that section of the country— underground, creeping, or a-wing—can be found in the Limberlost; but above all the birds.

Dainty green warblers nest in its tree-tops, and red-eyed vireos choose a location below. It is the home of bell-birds, finches, and thrushes. There are flocks of blackbirds, grackles, and crows. Jays and catbirds quarrel constantly, and marsh-wrens keep up never-ending chatter. Orioles swing their pendent purses from the branches, and with the tanagers picnic on mulberries and insects. In the evening, night-hawks dart on silent wing; whip-poorwills set up a plaintive cry that they continue far into the night; and owls revel in moonlight and rich hunting. At dawn, robins wake the echoes of each new day with the admonition, "Cheer up! Cheer up!" and a little later big black vultures go wheeling through cloudland or hang there, like frozen splashes, searching the Limberlost and the surrounding country for food. The boom of the bittern resounds all day, and above it the rasping scream of the blue heron, as he strikes terror to the hearts of frogdom; while the occasional cries of a lost loon, strayed from its flock in northern migration, fill the swamp with sounds of wailing.

Flashing through the tree-tops of the Limberlost there are birds whose colour is more brilliant than that of the gaudiest flower lifting its face to light and air. The lilies of the mire are not so white as the white herons that fish among them. The ripest spray of goldenrod is not so highly coloured as the burnished gold on the breast of the oriole that rocks on it. The jays are bluer than the calamus bed they wrangle above with throaty chatter. The finches are a finer purple than the ironwort. For every clump of foxfire flaming in the Limberlost, there is a cardinal glowing redder on a bush above it. These may not be more numerous than other birds, but their brilliant colouring and the fearless disposition make them seem so.

The Cardinal was hatched in a thicket of sweet-

7

brier and blackberry. His father was a tough old widower of many experiences and variable temper. He was the biggest, most aggressive redbird in the Limberlost, and easily reigned king of his kind. Catbirds, king-birds, and shrikes gave him a wide berth, and not even the ever-quarrelsome jays plucked up enough courage to antagonize him. A few days after his latest bereavement, he saw a fine, plump young female; and she so filled his eye that he gave her no rest until she permitted his caresses, and carried the first twig to the wild rose. She was very proud to mate with the king of the Limberlost; and if deep in her heart she felt transient fears of her lordly master, she gave no sign, for she was a bird of goodly proportion and fine feather herself.

She chose her location with the eye of an artist, and the judgment of a nest builder of more experience. It would be difficult for snakes and squirrels to penetrate that briery thicket. The white berry blossoms scarcely had ceased to attract a swarm of insects before the sweets of the roses recalled them; by the time they had faded, luscious big berries ripened within reach and drew food hunters. She built with far more than ordinary care. It was a beautiful nest, not nearly so carelessly made as those of her kindred all through the swamp. There was a distinct attempt at a cup shape, and it really was neatly lined with dried blades of sweet marsh grass. But it was in the laying of her first egg that the queen cardinal forever distinguished herself. She was a fine healthy bird, full of love and happiness over her first venture in nest-building, and she so far surpassed herself on that occasion she had difficulty in convincing any one that she was responsible for the result.

Indeed, she was compelled to lift beak and wing against her mate in defense of this egg, for it was so unusually large that he could not be persuaded short of force that some sneak of the feathered tribe had not slipped in and deposited it in her absence. The king felt sure there was something wrong with the egg, and wanted to roll it from the nest; but the queen knew her own, and stoutly battled for its protection. She further increased their prospects by laying three others. After that the king made up his mind that she was a most remarkable bird, and went away pleasure-seeking; but the queen settled to brooding, a picture of joyous faith and contentment.

Through all the long days, when the heat became intense, and the king was none too thoughtful of her appetite or comfort, she nestled those four eggs against her breast and patiently waited. The big egg was her treasure. She gave it constant care. Many times in a day she turned it; and always against her breast there was the individual pressure that distinguished it from the others. It was the first to hatch, of course, and the queen felt that she had enough if all the others failed her; for this egg pipped with a resounding pip, and before the silky down was really dry on the big terracotta body, the young Cardinal arose and lustily demanded food.

The king came to see him and at once acknowledged subjugation. He was the father of many promising cardinals, yet he never had seen one like this. He set the Limberlost echoes rolling with his jubilant rejoicing. He unceasingly hunted for the ripest berries and seed. He stuffed that baby from morning until night, and never came with food that he did not find him standing a-top the others calling for more. The queen was just as proud of him and quite as foolish in her idolatry, but she kept tally and gave the remainder every other worm in turn. They were unusually fine babies, but what chance has merely a fine baby in a family that possesses a prodigy? The Cardinal was as large as any two of the other nestlings, and so red the very down on him seemed tinged with crimson; his skin and even his feet were red.

He was the first to climb to the edge of the nest and the first to hop on a limb. He surprised his parents by finding a slug, and winged his first flight to such a distance that his adoring mother almost went into spasms lest his strength might fail, and he would fall into the swamp and become the victim of a hungry old turtle. He returned safely, however; and the king was so pleased he hunted him an unusually ripe berry, and perching before him, gave him his first language lesson. Of course, the Cardinal knew how to cry "Pee" and "Chee" when he burst his shell; but the king taught him to chip with accuracy and expression, and he learned that very day that male birds of the cardinal family always call "Chip," and the females "Chook." In fact, he learned so rapidly and was generally so observant, that before the king thought it wise to give the next lesson, he found him on a limb, his beak closed, his throat swelling, practising his own rendering of the tribal calls, "Wheat! Wheat! Wheat!" "Here! Here! Here!" and "Cheer! Cheer! Cheer!" This so delighted the king that he whistled them over and over and helped the youngster all he could.

He was so proud of him that this same night he gave him his first lesson in tucking his head properly and going to sleep alone. In a few more days, when he was sure of his wing strength, he gave him instructions in flying. He taught him how to spread his wings and slowly sail from tree to tree; how to fly in short broken curves, to avoid the aim of a hunter; how to turn abruptly in air and make a quick dash after a bug or an enemy. He taught him the proper angle at which to breast a stiff wind, and that he always should meet a storm head first, so that the water would run as the plumage lay.

His first bathing lesson was a pronounced success. The Cardinal enjoyed water like a duck. He bathed, splashed, and romped until his mother was almost crazy for fear he would attract a water-snake or turtle; but the element of fear was not a part of his disposition. He learned to dry, dress, and plume his feathers, and showed such remarkable pride in keeping himself immaculate, that although only a youngster, he was already a bird of such great promise, that many of the feathered inhabitants of the Limberlost came to pay him a call.

Next, the king took him on a long trip around the swamp, and taught him to select the proper places to hunt for worms; how to search under leaves for plant-lice and slugs for meat; which berries were good and safe, and the kind of weeds that bore the most and best seeds. He showed him how to find tiny pebbles to grind his food, and how to sharpen and polish his beak.

Then he took up the real music lessons, and taught him how to whistle and how to warble and trill. "Good Cheer! Good Cheer!" intoned the king. "Coo Cher! Coo Cher!" imitated the Cardinal. These songs were only studied repetitions, but there was a depth and volume in his voice that gave promise of future greatness, when age should have developed him, and experience awakened his emotions. He was an excellent musician for a youngster.

He soon did so well in caring for himself, in finding food and in flight, and grew so big and independent, that he made numerous excursions alone through the Limberlost; and so impressive were his proportions, and so aggressive his manner, that he suffered no molestation. In fact, the reign of the king promised to end speedily; but if he feared it he made no sign, and his pride in his wonderful offspring was always manifest. After the Cardinal had explored the swamp thoroughly, a longing for a wider range grew upon him; and day after day he lingered around the borders, looking across the wide cultivated fields, almost aching to test his wings in one long, high, wild stretch of flight.

A day came when the heat of the late summer set the marsh steaming, and the Cardinal, flying close to the borders, caught the breeze from the upland; and the vision of broad fields stretching toward the north so enticed him that he spread his wings, and following the line of trees and fences as much as possible, he made his first journey from home. That day was so delightful it decided his fortunes. It would seem that the swamp, so appreciated by his kindred, should have been sufficient for the Cardinal, but it was not. With every mile he winged his flight, came a greater sense of power and strength, and a keener love for the broad sweep of field and forest. His heart bounded with the zest of rocking on the wind, racing through the sunshine, and sailing over the endless panorama of waving corn fields, and woodlands.

The heat and closeness of the Limberlost seemed a prison well escaped, as on and on he flew in straight untiring flight. Crossing a field of half-ripened corn that sloped to the river, the Cardinal saw many birds feeding there, so he alighted on a tall tree to watch them. Soon he decided that he would like to try this new food. He found a place where a crow had left an ear nicely laid open, and clinging to the husk, as he saw the others do, he stretched to his full height and drove his strong sharp beak into the creamy grain. After the stifling swamp hunting, after the long exciting flight, to rock on this swaying corn and drink the rich milk of the grain, was to the Cardinal his first taste of nectar and ambrosia. He lifted his head when he came to the golden kernel, and chipping it in tiny specks, he tasted and approved with all the delight of an epicure in a delicious new dish.

16

Perhaps there were other treats in the next field. He decided to fly even farther. But he had gone only a short distance when he changed his course and turned to the South, for below him was a long, shining, creeping thing, fringed with willows, while towering above them were giant sycamore, maple, tulip, and elm trees that caught and rocked with the wind; and the Cardinal did not know what it was. Filled with wonder he dropped lower and lower. Birds were everywhere, many flying over and dipping into it; but its clear creeping silver was a mystery to the Cardinal.

The beautiful river of poetry and song that the Indians first discovered, and later with the French, named Ouabache; the winding shining river that Logan and Me-shin-go-me-sia loved; the only river that could tempt Wa-ca-co-nah from the Salamonie and Mississinewa; the river beneath whose silver sycamores and giant maples Chief Godfrey pitched his campfires, was never more beautiful than on that perfect autumn day.

With his feathers pressed closely, the Cardinal

alighted on a willow, and leaned to look, quivering with excitement and uttering explosive "chips"; for there he was, face to face with a big redbird that appeared neither peaceful nor timid. He uttered an impudent "Chip" of challenge, which, as it left his beak, was flung back to him. The Cardinal flared his crest and half lifted his wings, stiffening them at the butt; the bird he was facing did the same. In his surprise he arose to his full height with a dexterous little side step, and the other bird straightened and side-stepped exactly with him. This was too insulting for the Cardinal. Straining every muscle, he made a dash at the impudent stranger.

He struck the water with such force that it splashed above the willows, and a kingfisher, stationed on a stump opposite him, watching the shoals for minnows, saw it. He spread his beak and rolled forth rattling laughter, until his voice re-echoed from point to point down the river. The Cardinal scarcely knew how he got out, but he had learned a new lesson. That beautiful, shining, creeping thing was water; not thick, tepid, black marsh water, but pure, cool, silver water. He shook his plumage, feeling a degree redder from shame, but he would not be laughed into leaving. He found it too delightful. In a short time he ventured down and took a sip, and it was the first real drink of his life. Oh, but it was good!

When thirst from the heat and his long flight was quenched, he ventured in for a bath, and that was a new and delightful experience. How he splashed and splashed, and sent the silver drops flying! How he ducked and soaked and cooled in that rippling water, in which he might remain as long as he pleased and splash his fill; for he could see the bottom for a long distance all around, and easily could avoid anything attempting to harm him. He was so wet when his bath was finished he scarcely could reach a bush to dry and dress his plumage.

Once again in perfect feather, he remembered the bird of the water, and returned to the willow. There in the depths of the shining river the Cardinal discovered himself, and his heart swelled big with just pride. Was that broad full breast his? Where had he seen any other cardinal with a crest so high it waved in the wind? How big and black his eyes were, and his beard was almost as long and crisp as his father's. He spread his wings and gloated on their sweep, and twisted and flirted his tail. He went over his toilet again and dressed every feather on him. He scoured the back of his neck with the butt of his wings, and tucking his head under them, slowly drew it out time after time to polish his crest. He turned and twisted. He rocked and paraded, and every glimpse he caught of his size and beauty filled him with pride. He strutted like a peacock and chattered like a jay.

When he could find no further points to admire, something else caught his attention. When he "chipped" there was an answering "Chip" across the river; certainly there was no cardinal there, so it must be that he was hearing his own voice as well as seeing himself. Selecting a conspicuous perch he sent an incisive "Chip!" across the water, and in kind it came back to him. Then he "chipped" softly and tenderly, as he did in the Limberlost to a favourite little sister who often came and perched beside him in the maple where he slept, and softly and tenderly came the answer. Then the Cardinal understood. "Wheat! Wheat! Wheat!" He whistled it high, and he whistled it low. "Cheer! Cheer! Cheer!" He whistled it tenderly and sharply and imperiously. "Here! Here! Here!" At this ringing command, every bird, as far as the river carried his voice, came to investigate and remained to admire. Over and over he rang every change he could invent. He made a gallant effort at warbling and trilling, and then, with the gladdest heart he ever had known, he burst into ringing song: "Good Cheer! Good Cheer! Good Cheer!"

As evening came on he grew restless and uneasy, so he slowly winged his way back to the Limberlost; but that day forever spoiled him for a swamp bird. In the night he restlessly ruffled his feathers, and sniffed for the breeze of the meadows. He tasted the corn and the clear water again. He admired his image in the river, and longed for the sound of his voice, until he began murmuring, "Wheat! Wheat! Wheat!" in his sleep. In the earliest dawn a robin awoke him singing, "Cheer up! Cheer up!" and he answered with a sleepy "Cheer! Cheer! Cheer!" Later the robin sang again with exquisite softness and tenderness: "Cheer up, Dearie! Cheer up, Dearie! Cheer up! Cheer up! Cheer!" The Cardinal, now fully awakened, shouted lustily, "Good Cheer! Good Cheer!" and after that it was only a short time until he was on his way toward the shining river. It was better than before, and every following day found him feasting in the corn field and bathing in the shining water; but he always returned to his family at nightfall.

When black frosts began to strip the Limberlost, and food was almost reduced to dry seed, there came a day on which the king marshalled his followers and gave the magic signal. With dusk he led them southward, mile after mile, until their breath fell short, and their wings ached with unaccustomed flight; but because of the trips to the river, the Cardinal was stronger than the others, and he easily kept abreast of the king. In the early morning, even before the robins were awake, the king settled in the Everglades. But the Cardinal had lost all liking for swamp life, so he stubbornly set out alone, and in a short time he had found another river. It was not quite so delightful as the shining river; but still it was beautiful, and on its gently sloping bank was an orange orchard. There the Cardinal rested, and found a winter home after his heart's desire.

The following morning, a golden-haired little girl and an old man with snowy locks came hand in hand through the orchard. The child saw the redbird and immediately claimed him, and that same day the edict went forth that a very dreadful time was in store for any one who harmed or even frightened the Cardinal. So in security began a series of days that were pure delight. The orchard was alive with insects, attracted by the heavy odours, and slugs infested the bark. Feasting was almost as good as in the Limberlost, and always there was the river to drink from and to splash in at will.

In those days the child and the old man lingered for hours in the orchard, watching the bird that every day seemed to grow bigger and brighter. What a picture his coat, now a bright cardinal red, made against the waxy green leaves! How big and brilliant he seemed as he raced and darted in play among the creamy blossoms! How the little girl stood with clasped hands worshipping him, as with swelling throat he rocked on the highest spray and sang his inspiring chorus over and over: "Good Cheer! Good Cheer!" Every day they came to watch and listen. They scattered crumbs; and the Cardinal grew so friendly that he greeted their coming with a quick "Chip! Chip!" while the delighted child tried to repeat it after him. Soon they became such friends that when he saw them approaching he would call softly "Chip! Chip!"

24

and then with beady eyes and tilted head await her reply.

Sometimes a member of his family from the Everglades found his way into the orchard, and the Cardinal, having grown to feel a sense of proprietorship, resented the intrusion and pursued him like a streak of flame. Whenever any straggler had this experience, he returned to the swamp realizing that the Cardinal of the orange orchard was almost twice his size and strength, and so startlingly red as to be a wonder.

One day a gentle breeze from the north sprang up and stirred the orange branches, wafting the heavy perfume across the land and out to sea, and spread in its stead a cool, delicate, pungent odour. The Cardinal lifted his head and whistled an inquiring note. He was not certain, and went on searching for slugs, and predicting happiness in full round notes: "Good Cheer! Good Cheer!" Again the odour swept the orchard, so strong that this time there was no mistaking it. The Cardinal darted to the topmost branch, his crest flaring, his tail twitching nervously. "Chip! Chip!" he cried with excited insistence, "Chip! Chip!"

The breeze was coming stiffly and steadily now, unlike anything the Cardinal ever had known, for its cool breath told of ice-bound fields breaking up under the sun. Its damp touch was from the spring showers washing the face of the northland. Its subtle odour was the commingling of myriads of unfolding leaves and crisp plants, upspringing; its pungent perfume was the pollen of catkins.

Up in the land of the Limberlost, old Mother Nature, with strident muttering, had set about her annual house cleaning. With her efficient broom, the March wind, she was sweeping every nook and cranny clean. With her scrub-bucket overflowing with April showers, she was washing the face of all creation, and if these measures failed to produce cleanliness to her satisfaction, she gave a final polish with storms of hail. The shining river was filled to overflowing; breaking up the ice and carrying a load of refuse, it went rolling to the sea. The ice and snow had not altogether gone; but

26

the long-pregnant earth was mothering her children. She cringed at every step, for the ground was teeming with life. Bug and worm were working to light and warmth. Thrusting aside the mold and leaves above them, spring beauties, hepaticas, and violets lifted tender golden-green heads. The sap was flowing, and leafless trees were covered with swelling buds. Delicate mosses were creeping over every stick of decaying timber. The lichens on stone and fence were freshly painted in unending shades of gray and green. Myriads of flowers and vines were springing up to cover last year's decaying leaves. "The beautiful uncut hair of graves" was creeping over meadow, spreading beside roadways, and blanketing every naked spot.

The Limberlost was waking to life even ahead of the fields and the river. Through the winter it had been the barest and dreariest of places; but now the earliest signs of returning spring were in its martial music, for when the green hyla pipes, and the bullfrog drums, the bird voices soon join them. The catkins bloomed first; and then, in an incredibly short time, flags, rushes, and vines were like a sea of waving green, and swelling buds were ready to burst. In the upland the smoke was curling over sugar-camp and clearing; in the forests animals were rousing from their long sleep; the shad were starting anew their never-ending journey up the shining river; peeps of green were mantling hilltop and valley; and the northland was ready for its dearest springtime treasures to come home again.

From overhead were ringing those first glad notes, caught nearer the Throne than those of any other bird, "Spring o' year! Spring o' year!"; while stilt-legged little killdeers were scudding around the Limberlost and beside the river, flinging from cloudland their "Kill deer! Kill deer!" call. The robins in the orchards were pulling the long dried blades of last year's grass from beneath the snow to line their mud-walled cups; and the bluebirds were at the hollow apple tree. Flat on the top rail, the doves were gathering their few coarse sticks and twigs together. It was such a splendid place to set their cradle. The weatherbeaten, rotting old rails were the very colour of the busy dove mother. Her red-rimmed eye fitted into the background like a tiny scarlet lichen cup. Surely no one would ever see her! The Limberlost and shining river, the fields and forests, the wayside bushes and fences, the stumps, logs, hollow trees, even the bare brown breast of Mother Earth, were all waiting to cradle their own again; and by one of the untold miracles each would return to its place.

There was intoxication in the air. The subtle, pungent, ravishing odours on the wind, of unfolding leaves, ice-water washed plants, and catkin pollen, were an elixir to humanity. The cattle of the field were fairly drunk with it, and herds, dry-fed during the winter, were coming to their first grazing with heads thrown high, romping, bellowing, and racing like wild things.

The north wind, sweeping from icy fastnesses, caught this odour of spring, and carried it to the orange orchards and Everglades; and at a breath of it, crazed with excitement, the Cardinal went flaming through the orchard, for with no one to teach him, he knew what it meant. The call had come. Holidays were over.

It was time to go home, time to riot in crisp freshness, time to go courting, time to make love, time to possess his own, time for mating and nest-building. All that day he flashed around, nervous with dread of the unknown, and palpitant with delightful expectation; but with the coming of dusk he began his journey northward.

When he passed the Everglades, he winged his way slowly, and repeatedly sent down a challenging "Chip," but there was no answer. Then the Cardinal knew that the north wind had carried a true message, for the king and his followers were ahead of him on their way to the Limberlost. Mile after mile, a thing of pulsing fire, he breasted the blue-black night, and it was not so very long until he could discern a flickering patch of darkness sweeping the sky before him. The Cardinal flew steadily in a straight sweep, until with a throb of triumph in his heart, he arose in his course, and from far overhead, flung down a boastful challenge to the king and his followers, as he sailed above them and was lost from sight.

It was still dusky with the darkness of night when he crossed the Limberlost, dropping low enough to see its branches laid bare, to catch a gleam of green in its swelling buds, and to hear the wavering chorus of its frogs. But there was no hesitation in his flight. Straight and sure he winged his way toward the shining river; and it was only a few more miles until the rolling waters of its springtime flood caught his eye. Dropping precipitately, he plunged his burning beak into the loved water; then he flew into a fine old stag sumac and tucked his head under his wing for a short rest. He had made the long flight in one unbroken sweep, and he was sleepy. In utter content he ruffled his feathers and closed his eyes, for he was beside the shining river; and it would be another season before the orange orchard would ring again with his "Good Cheer! Good Cheer!"

*"Wet year! Wet year!" prophesied
the Cardinal*

II

"Wet year! Wet year!" prophesied the Cardinal

THE sumac seemed to fill his idea of a perfect location from the very first. He perched on a limb, and between dressing his plumage and pecking at last year's sour dried berries, he sent abroad his prediction. Old Mother Nature verified his wisdom by sending a dashing shower, but he cared not at all for a wetting. He knew how to turn his crimson suit into the most perfect of water-proof coats; so he flattened his crest, sleeked his feathers, and breasting the April downpour, kept on calling for rain. He knew he would appear brighter when it was past, and he seemed to know, too, that every

35

day of sunshine and shower would bring nearer his heart's desire.

He was a very Beau Brummel while he waited. From morning until night he bathed, dressed his feathers, sunned himself, fluffed and flirted. He strutted and "chipped" incessantly. He claimed that sumac for his very own, and stoutly battled for possession with many intruders. It grew on a densely wooded slope, and the shining river went singing between grassy banks, whitened with spring beauties, below it. Crowded around it were thickets of papaw, wild grape-vines, thorn, dogwood, and red haw, that attracted bug and insect; and just across the old snake fence was a field of mellow mould sloping to the river, that soon would be plowed for corn, turning out numberless big fat grubs.

He was compelled almost hourly to wage battles for his location, for there was something fine about the old stag sumac that attracted homestead seekers. A sober pair of robins began laying their foundations there the morning the Cardinal ar-

rived, and a couple of blackbirds tried to take possession before the day had passed. He had little
trouble with the robins. They were easily con-
quered, and with small protest settled a rod up
the bank in a wild-plum tree; but the air was thick
with "chips," chatter, and red and black feathers,
before the blackbirds acknowledged defeat. They
were old-timers, and knew about the grubs and
the young corn; but they also knew when they
were beaten, so they moved down stream to a
scrub oak, trying to assure each other that it was
the place they really had wanted from the first.

The Cardinal was left boasting and strutting in
the sumac, but in his heart he found it lonesome
business. Being the son of a king, he was much too
dignified to beg for a mate, and besides, it took all
his time to guard the sumac; but his eyes were
wide open to all that went on around him, and he
envied the blackbird his glossy, devoted little
sweetheart, with all his might. He almost strained
his voice trying to rival the love-song of a skylark
that hung among the clouds above a meadow

across the river, and poured down to his mate a story of adoring love and sympathy. He screamed a "Chip" of such savage jealousy at a pair of kill-deer lovers that he sent them scampering down the river bank without knowing that the crime of which they stood convicted was that of being mated when he was not. As for the doves that were already brooding on the line fence beneath the maples, the Cardinal was torn between two opinions.

He was alone, he was love-sick, and he was holding the finest building location beside the shining river for his mate, and her slowness in coming made their devotion difficult to endure when he coveted a true love; but it seemed to the Cardinal that he never could so forget himself as to emulate the example of that dove lover. The dove had no dignity; he was so effusive he was a nuisance. He kept his dignified Quaker mate stuffed to discomfort; he clung to the side of the nest trying to help brood until he almost crowded her from the eggs. He pestered her with caresses and cooed over his love-song until every chipmunk on the line fence was familiar with his story. The Cardinal's temper was worn to such a fine edge that he darted at the dove one day and pulled a big tuft of feathers from his back. When he had returned to the sumac, he was compelled to admit that his anger lay quite as much in that he had no one to love as because the dove was disgustingly devoted.

Every morning brought new arrivals—trim young females fresh from their long holiday, and big boastful males appearing their brightest and bravest, each singer almost splitting his throat in the effort to captivate the mate he coveted. They came flashing down the river bank, like rockets of scarlet, gold, blue, and black; rocking on the willows, splashing in the water, bursting into jets of melody, making every possible display of their beauty and music; and at times fighting fiercely when they discovered that the females they were wooing favoured their rivals and desired only to be friendly with them.

The heart of the Cardinal sank as he watched.

There was not a member of his immediate family among them. He pitied himself as he wondered if fate had in store for him the trials he saw others suffering. Those dreadful feathered females! How they coquetted! How they flirted! How they sleeked and flattened their plumage, and with half-open beaks and sparkling eyes, hopped closer and closer as if charmed. The eager singers, with swelling throats, sang and sang in a very frenzy of extravagant pleading, but just when they felt sure their little loves were on the point of surrender, a rod distant above the bushes would go streaks of feathers, and there was nothing left but to endure the bitter disappointment, follow them, and begin all over. For the last three days the Cardinal had been watching his cousin, rose-breasted Grosbeak, make violent love to the most exquisite little female, who apparently encouraged his advances, only to see him left sitting as blue and disconsolate as any human lover, when he discovers that the maid who has coquetted with him for a season belongs to another man.

The Cardinal flew to the very top of the highest sycamore and looked across country toward the Limberlost. Should he go there seeking a swamp mate among his kindred? It was not an endurable thought. To be sure, matters were becoming serious. No bird beside the shining river had plumed, paraded, or made more music than he. Was it all to be wasted? By this time he confidently had expected results. Only that morning he had swelled with pride as he heard Mrs. Jay tell her quarrelsome husband that she wished she could exchange him for the Cardinal. Did not the gentle dove pause by the sumac, when she left brooding to take her morning dip in the dust, and gaze at him with unconcealed admiration? No doubt she devoutly wished her plain pudgy husband wore a scarlet coat. But it is praise from one's own sex that is praise indeed, and only an hour ago the lark had reported that from his lookout above cloud he saw no other singer anywhere so splendid as the Cardinal of the sumac. Because of these things he held fast to his conviction that he was a prince indeed; and he decided to remain in his chosen location and with his physical and vocal attractions compel the finest little cardinal in the fields to seek him.

He planned it all very carefully: how she would hear his splendid music and come to take a peep at him; how she would be captivated by his size and beauty; how she would come timidly, but come, of course, for his approval; how he would condescend to accept her if she pleased him in all particulars; how she would be devoted to him; and how she would approve his choice of a home, for the sumac was in a lovely spot for scenery, as well as nest-building. For several days he had boasted, he had bantered, he had challenged, he had on this last day almost condescended to coaxing, but not one little bright-eyed cardinal female had come to offer herself.

The performance of a brown thrush drove him wild with envy. The thrush came gliding up the river bank, a rusty-coated, sneaking thing of the underbrush, and taking possession of a thorn bush just opposite the sumac, he sang for an hour in the open. There was no way to improve that music. It was woven fresh from the warp and woof of his fancy. It was a song so filled with the joy and gladness of spring, notes so thrilled with love's pleading and passion's tender pulsing pain, that at its close there were a half-dozen admiring thrush females gathered around. With care and deliberation the brown thrush selected the most attractive, and she followed him to the thicket as if charmed.

It was the Cardinal's dream materialized for another before his very eyes, and it filled him with envy. If that plain brown bird that slinked as if he had a theft to account for, could, by showing himself and singing for an hour, win a mate, why should not he, the most gorgeous bird of the woods, openly flaunting his charms and discoursing his music, have at least equal success? Should he, the proudest, most magnificent of cardinals, be compelled to go seeking a mate like any common bird? Perish the thought!

He went to the river to bathe. After finding a

spot where the water flowed crystal-clear over a bed of white limestone, he washed until he felt that he could be no cleaner. Then the Cardinal went to his favourite sun-parlour, and stretching on a limb, he stood his feathers on end, and sunned, fluffed and prinked until he was immaculate.

On the tip-top antler of the old stag sumac, he perched and strained until his jetty whiskers appeared stubby. He poured out a tumultuous cry vibrant with every passion raging in him. He caught up his own rolling echoes and changed and varied them. He improvised, and set the shining river ringing, "Wet year! Wet year!"

He whistled and whistled until all birdland and even mankind heard, for the farmer paused at his kitchen door, with his pails of foaming milk, and called to his wife:

"Hear that, Maria! Jest hear it! I swanny, if that bird doesn't stop predictin' wet weather, I'll get so scared I won't durst put in my corn afore June. They's some birds like killdeers an' bobwhites 'at can make things pretty plain, but I never heard a bird 'at could jest speak words out clear an' distinct like that fellow. Seems to come from the river bottom. B'lieve I'll jest step down that way an' see if the lower field is ready for the plow yet."

"Abram Johnson," said his wife, "bein's you set up for an honest man, if you want to trapse through slush an' drizzle a half-mile to see a bird, why say so, but don't for land's sake lay it on to plowin' 'at you know in all conscience won't be ready for a week yet 'thout pretendin' to look."

Abram grinned sheepishly. "I'm willin' to call it the bird if you are, Maria. I've been hearin' him from the barn all day, an' there's somethin' kind o' human in his notes 'at takes me jest a little diffrunt from any other bird I ever noticed. I'm really curious to set eyes on him. Seemed to me from his singin' out to the barn, it 'ud be mighty near like meetin' folks."

"Bosh!" exclaimed Maria. "I don't s'pose he sings a mite better 'an any other bird. It's jest the

45

old Wabash rollin' up the echoes. A bird singin' beside the river always sounds twicet as fine as one on the hills. I've knowed that for forty year. Chances are 'at he'll be gone 'fore you get there.''

As Abram opened the door, "Wet year! Wet year!" pealed the flaming prophet.

He went out, closing the door softly, and with an utter disregard for the corn field, made a bee line for the musician.

"I don't know as this is the best for twinges o' rheumatiz," he muttered, as he turned up his collar and drew his old hat lower to keep the splashing drops from his face. "I don't jest rightly s'pose I should go; but I'm free to admit I'd as lief be dead as not to answer when I get a call, an' the fact is, I'm *called* down beside the river."

"Wet year! Wet year!" rolled the Cardinal's prediction.

"Thanky, old fellow! Glad to hear you! Didn't jest need the information, but I got my bearin's rightly from it! I can about pick out your bush, an' it's well along towards evenin', too, an' must be mighty near your bedtime. Looks as if you might be stayin' round these parts! I'd like it powerful well if you'd settle right here, say 'bout where you are. An' where are you, anyway?"

Abram went peering and dodging beside the fence, peeping into the bushes, searching for the bird. Suddenly there was a whir of wings and a streak of crimson.

"Scared you into the next county, I s'pose," he muttered.

But it came nearer being a scared man than a frightened bird, for the Cardinal flashed straight toward him until only a few yards away, and then, swaying on a bush, it chipped, cheered, peeked, whistled broken notes, and manifested perfect delight at the sight of the white-haired old man. Abram stared in astonishment.

"Lord A'mighty!" he gasped. "Big as a blackbird, red as a live coal, an' a-comin' right at me. You are somebody's pet, that's what you are! An' no, you ain't either. Settin' on a sawed stick in a little wire house takes all the ginger out of any

47

bird, an' their feathers are always mussy. Inside o' a cage never saw you, for they ain't a feather out o' place on you. You are finer'n a piece o' red satin. An' you got that way o' swingin' an' dancin' an' high-steppin' right out in God A'mighty's big woods, a teeterin' in the wind, an' a dartin' 'crost the water. Cage never touched you! But you are somebody's pet jest the same. An' I look like the man, an' you are tryin' to tell me so, by gum!"

Leaning toward Abram, the Cardinal turned his head from side to side, and peered, "chipped," and waited for an answering "Chip" from a little golden-haired child, but there was no way for the man to know that.

"It's jest as sure as fate," he said. "You think you know me, an' you are tryin' to tell me somethin'. Wish to land I knowed what you want! Are you tryin' to tell me 'Howdy'? Well, I don't 'low nobody to be politer 'an I am, so far as I know."

Abram lifted his old hat, and the raindrops glistened on his white hair. He squared his shoulders and stood very erect.

48

"Howdy, Mr. Redbird! How d'ye find yerself this evenin'? I don't jest riccolict ever seein' you before, but I'll never meet you agin 'thout knowin' you. When d'you arrive? Come through by the special midnight flyer, did you? Well, you never was more welcome any place in your life. I'd give a right smart sum this minnit if you'd say you came to settle on this river bank. How do you like it? To my mind it's jest as near Paradise as you'll strike on earth.

"Old Wabash is a twister for curvin' and windin' round, an' it's limestone bed half the way, an' the water's as pretty an' clear as in Maria's springhouse. An' as for trimmin', why say, Mr. Redbird, I'll jest leave it to you if she ain't all trimmed up like a woman's spring bunnit. Look at the grass a-creepin' right down till it's a trailin' in the water! Did you ever see jest quite such fine fringy willers? An' you wait a little, an' the flowerin' mallows 'at grows long the shinin' old river are fine as garden hollyhocks. Maria says 'at they'd be purtier 'an hers if they were only double; but,

49

Lord, Mr. Redbird, they are! See 'em once on the bank, an' agin in the water! An' back a little an' there's jest thickets of papaw, an' thorns, an' wild grape-vines, an' crab, an' red an' black haw, an' dogwood, an' sumac, an' spicebush, an' trees! Lord! Mr. Redbird, the sycamores, an' maples, an' tulip, an' ash, an' elm trees are so bustin' fine 'long the old Wabash they put 'em into poetry books an' sing songs about 'em. What do you think o' that? Jest back o' you a little there's a sycamore split into five trunks, any one o' them a famous big tree, tops up 'mong the clouds, an' roots diggin' under the old river; an' over a little farther's a maple 'at's eight big trees in one. Most anything you can name, you can find it 'long this ole Wabash, if you only know where to hunt for it.

"They's mighty few white men takes the trouble to look, but the Indians used to know. They'd come canoein' an' fishin' down the river an' camp under these very trees, an' Ma 'ud git so mad at the old squaws. Settlers wasn't so thick then, an' you had to be mighty careful not to rile 'em, an'

they'd come a-trapesin' with their wild berries.
Woods full o' berries! Anybody could get 'em by
the bushel for the pickin', an' we hadn't got on to
raisin' much wheat, an' had to carry it on horses
over into Ohio to get it milled. Took Pa five days
to make the trip; an' then the blame old squaws
'ud come, an' Ma 'ud be compelled to hand over
to 'em her big white loaves. Jest about set her
plumb crazy. Used to get up in the night, an' fix
her yeast, an' bake, an' let the oven cool, an' hide
the bread out in the wheat bin, an' get the smell
of it all out o' the house by good daylight, so's 'at
she could say there wasn't a loaf in the cabin. Oh!
if it's good pickin' you're after, they's berries for
all creation 'long the river yet; an' jest wait a few
days till old April gets done showerin' an' I plow
this corn field!"

Abram set a foot on the third rail and leaned
his elbows on the top. The Cardinal chipped de-
lightedly and hopped and tilted closer.

"I hadn't jest 'lowed all winter I'd tackle this
field again. I've turned it every spring for forty

51

year. Bought it when I was a young fellow, jest married to Maria. Shouldered a big debt on it; but I always loved these slopin' fields, an' my share of this old Wabash hasn't been for sale nor tradin' any time this past forty year. I've hung on to it like grim death, for it's jest that much o' Paradise I'm plumb sure of. First time I plowed this field, Mr. Redbird, I only hit the high places. Jest married Maria, an' I didn't touch earth any too frequent all that summer. I've plowed it every year since, an' I've been 'lowin' all this winter, when the rheumatiz was gettin' in its work, 'at I'd give it up this spring an' turn it to medder; but I don't know. Once I got started, b'lieve I could go it all right an'. not feel it so much, if you'd stay to cheer me up a little an' post me on the weather. Hate the doggondest to own I'm worsted, an' if you say it's stay, b'lieve I'll try it. Very sight o' you kinder warms the cockles o' my heart all up, an' every skip you take sets me a-wantin' to be jumpin', too.

"What on earth are you lookin' for? Man! I b'lieve it's grub! Somebody's been feedin' you!

An' you want me to keep it up? Well, you struck it all right, Mr. Redbird. Feed you? You bet I will! You needn't even 'rastle for grubs if you don't want to. Like as not you're feelin' hungry right now, pickin' bein' so slim these airly days. Land's sake! I hope you don't feel you've come too soon. I'll fetch you everything on the place it's likely a redbird ever teched, airly in the mornin' if you'll say you'll stay an' wave your torch 'long my river bank this summer. I haven't a scrap about me now. Yes, I have, too! Here's a handful o' corn I was takin' to the banty rooster; but shucks! he's fat as a young shoat now. Corn's a leetle big an' hard for you. Mebby I can split it up a mite."

Abram took out his jack-knife, and dotting a row of grains along the top rail, he split and shaved them down as fine as possible; and as he reached one end of the rail, the Cardinal, with a spasmodic "Chip!" dashed down and snatched a particle from the other, and flashed back to the bush, tested, approved, and chipped his thanks.

"Pshaw now!" said Abram, staring wide-eyed.

53

"Doesn't that beat you? So you really are a pet? Best kind of a pet in the whole world, too! Makin' everybody 'at sees you happy, an' havin' some chance to be happy yourself. An' I look like your friend? Well! Well! I'm monstrous willin' to adopt you if you'll take me; an', as for feedin', from to-morrow on I'll find time to set your little table 'long this same rail every day. I s'pose Maria 'ull say 'at I'm gone plumb crazy; but, for that matter, if I ever get her down to see you jest once, the trick's done with her, too, for you're the prettiest thing God ever made in the shape of a bird, 'at I ever saw. Look at that topknot a wavin' in the wind! Maybe praise to the face is open disgrace; but I'll take your share an' mine, too, an' tell you right here an' now 'at you're the blamedest prettiest thing 'at I ever saw.

"But Lord! You ortn't be so careless! Don't you know you ain't nothin' but jest a target? Why don't you keep out o' sight a little? You come a-shinneyin' up to nine out o' ten men 'long the river like this, an' your purty, coaxin', palaverin' way won't save a feather on you. You'll get the little red heart shot plumb outen your little red body, an' that's what you'll get. It's a dratted shame! An' there's law to protect you, too. They's a good big fine for killin' such as you, but nobody seems to push it. Every fool wants to test his aim, an' you're the brightest thing on the river bank for a mark.

"Well, if you'll stay right where you are, it 'ull be a sorry day for any cuss 'at teches you; 'at I'll promise you, Mr. Redbird. This land's mine, an' if you locate on it, you're mine till time to go back to that other old fellow 'at looks like me. Wonder if he's any willinger to feed you an' stand up for you 'an I am?"

"Here! Here! Here!" whistled the Cardinal.

"Well, I'm mighty glad if you're sayin' you'll stay! Guess it will be all right if you don't meet some o' them Limberlost hens an' tole off to the swamp. Lord! the Limberlost ain't to be compared with the river, Mr. Redbird. You're foolish if you go! Talkin' 'bout goin', I must be goin' myself, or

Maria will be comin' down the line fence with the lantern; an', come to think of it, I'm a little moist, not to say downright damp. But then you *warned* me, didn't you, old fellow? Well, I told Maria seein' you 'ud be like meetin' folks, an' it has been. Good deal more'n I counted on, an' I've talked more'n I have in a whole year. Hardly think now 'at I've the reputation o' being a mighty quiet fellow, would you?"

Abram straightened and touched his hat brim in a trim half military salute. "Well, good-bye, Mr. Redbird. Never had more pleasure meetin' anybody in my life 'cept first time I met Maria. You think about the plowin', an', if you say 'stay,' it's a go! Good-bye; an' do be a little more careful o' yourself. See you in the mornin', right after breakfast, no count taken o' the weather."

"Wet year! Wet year!" called the Cardinal after his retreating figure.

Abram turned and gravely saluted the second time. The Cardinal went to the top rail and feasted on the sweet grains of corn until his craw was full, and then nestled in the sumac and went to sleep. Early next morning he was abroad and in fine toilet, and with a full voice from the top of the sumac greeted the day—"Wet year! Wet year!"

Far down the river echoed his voice until it so closely resembled some member of his family replying that he followed, searching the banks mile after mile on either side, until finally he heard voices of his kind. He located them, but it was only several staid old couples, a long time mated, and busy with their nest-building. The Cardinal returned to the sumac, feeling a degree lonelier than ever.

He decided to prospect in the opposite direction, and taking wing, he started up the river. Following the channel, he winged his flight for miles over the cool sparkling water, between the tangle of foliage bordering the banks. When he came to the long cumbrous structures of wood with which men had bridged the river, where the shuffling feet of tired farm horses raised clouds of dust and set the echoes rolling with their thunderous hoof beats, he was afraid; and rising high, he sailed over them in short broken curves of flight. But where giant maple and ash, leaning, locked branches across the channel in one of old Mother Nature's bridges for the squirrels, he knew no fear, and dipped so low beneath them that his image trailed a wavering shadow on the silver path he followed.

He rounded curve after curve, and frequently stopping on a conspicuous perch, flung a ringing challenge in the face of the morning. With every mile the way he followed grew more beautiful. The river bed was limestone, and the swiftly flowing water, clear and limpid. The banks were precipitate in some places, gently sloping in others, and always crowded with a tangle of foliage.

At an abrupt curve in the river he mounted to the summit of a big ash and made boastful prophecy, "Wet year! Wet year!" and on all sides there sprang up the voices of his kind. Startled, the Cardinal took wing. He followed the river in a circling flight until he remembered that here might be the opportunity to win the coveted river mate, and going slower to select the highest branch on which to display his charms, he discovered that he was only a few yards from the ash from which he had made his prediction. The Cardinal flew over the narrow neck and sent another call, then without awaiting a reply, again he flashed up the river and circled Horseshoe Bend. When he came to the same ash for the third time, he understood.

The river circled in one great curve. The Cardinal mounted to the tip-top limb of the ash and looked around him. There was never a fairer sight for the eye of man or bird. The mist and shimmer of early spring were in the air. The Wabash rounded Horseshoe Bend in a silver circle, rimmed by a tangle of foliage bordering both its banks; and inside lay a low open space covered with waving marsh grass and the blue bloom of sweet calamus. Scattered around were mighty trees, but conspicuous above any, in the very center, was a giant sycamore, split at its base into three large trees, whose waving branches seemed to sweep the face of heaven, and whose roots, like miserly fingers, clutched deep into the black muck of Rainbow Bottom.

It was in this lovely spot that the rainbow at last materialized, and at its base, free to all humanity who cared to seek, the Great Alchemist had left His rarest treasures—the gold of sunshine, diamond water-drops, emerald foliage, and sapphire sky. For good measure, there were added seeds, berries, and insects for the birds; and wild flowers, fruit, and nuts for the children. Above all, the sycamore waved its majestic head.

It made a throne that seemed suitable for the son of the king; and mounting to its topmost branch, for miles the river carried his challenge: "Ho, cardinals! Look this way! Behold me! Have you seen any other of so great size? Have you any to equal my grace? Who can whistle so loud, so clear, so compelling a note? Who will fly to me for protection? Who will come and be my mate?"

He flared his crest high, swelled his throat with

rolling notes, and appeared so big and brilliant that among the many cardinals that had gathered to hear, there was not one to compare with him.

Black envy filled their hearts. Who was this flaming dashing stranger, flaunting himself in the faces of their females? There were many unmated cardinals in Rainbow Bottom, and many jealous males. A second time the Cardinal, rocking and flashing, proclaimed himself; and there was a note of feminine approval so strong that he caught it. Tilting on a twig, his crest flared to full height, his throat swelled to bursting, his heart too big for his body, the Cardinal shouted his challenge for the third time; when clear and sharp arose a cry in answer, "Here! Here! Here!" It came from a female that had accepted the caresses of the brightest cardinal in Rainbow Bottom only the day before, and had spent the morning carrying twigs to a thicket of red haws.

The Cardinal, with a royal flourish, sprang in air to seek her; but her outraged mate was ahead of him, and with a scream she fled, leaving a tuft of feathers in her mate's beak. In turn the Cardinal struck him like a flashing rocket, and then red war waged in Rainbow Bottom. The females scattered for cover with all their might. The Cardinal worked in a kiss on one poor little bird, too frightened to escape him; then the males closed in, and serious business began. The Cardinal would have enjoyed a fight vastly with two or three opponents; but a half-dozen made discretion better than valour. He darted among them, scattering them right and left, and made for the sycamore. With all his remaining breath, he insolently repeated his challenge; and then headed down stream for the sumac with what grace he could command.

There was an hour of angry recrimination before sweet peace brooded again in Rainbow Bottom. The newly mated pair finally made up; the females speedily resumed their coquetting, and forgot the captivating stranger—all save the poor little one that had been kissed by accident. She never had been kissed before, and never had expected that she would be, for she was a creature of many misfortunes of every nature.

She had been hatched from a fifth egg to begin with; and every one knows the disadvantage of beginning life with four sturdy older birds on top of one. It was a meager egg, and a feeble baby that pipped its shell. The remainder of the family stood and took nearly all the food so that she almost starved in the nest, and she never really knew the luxury of a hearty meal until her elders had flown. That lasted only a few days; for the others went then, and their parents followed them so far afield that the poor little soul, clamouring alone in the nest, almost perished. Hunger-driven, she climbed to the edge and exercised her wings until she managed some sort of flight to a neighbouring bush. She missed the twig and fell to the ground, where she lay cold and shivering.

She cried pitifully, and was almost dead when a brown-faced, barefoot boy, with a fishing-pole on his shoulder, passed and heard her.

"Poor little thing, you are almost dead," he said.

63

"I know what I'll do with you. I'll take you over and set you in the bushes where I heard those other redbirds, and then your ma will feed you."

The boy turned back and carefully set her on a limb close to one of her brothers, and there she got just enough food to keep her alive.

So her troubles continued. Once a squirrel chased her, and she saved herself by crowding into a hole so small her pursuer could not follow. The only reason she escaped a big blue racer when she went to take her first bath, was that a hawk had his eye on the snake and snapped it up at just the proper moment to save the poor, quivering little bird. She was left so badly frightened that she could not move for a long time.

All the tribulations of birdland fell to her lot. She was so frail and weak she lost her family in migration, and followed with some strangers that were none too kind. Life in the South had been full of trouble. Once a bullet grazed her so closely she lost two of her wing quills, and that made her more timid than ever. Coming North, she had

64

given out again and finally had wandered into Rainbow Bottom, lost and alone.

She was such a shy, fearsome little body, the females all flouted her; and the males never seemed to notice that there was material in her for a very fine mate. Every other female cardinal in Rainbow Bottom had several males courting her, but this poor, frightened, lonely one had never a suitor; and she needed love so badly! Now she had been kissed by this magnificent stranger!

Of course, she knew it really was not her kiss. He had intended it for the bold creature that had answered his challenge, but since it came to her, it was hers, in a way, after all. She hid in the underbrush for the remainder of the day, and was never so frightened in all her life. She brooded over it constantly, and morning found her at the down curve of the horseshoe, straining her ears for the rarest note she ever had heard. All day she hid and waited, and the following days were filled with longing, but he never came again.

So one morning, possessed with courage she did

not understand, and filled with longing that drove her against her will, she started down the river. For miles she sneaked through the underbrush, and watched and listened; until at last night came, and she returned to Rainbow Bottom. The next morning she set out early and flew to the spot from which she had turned back the night before. From there she glided through the bushes and underbrush, trembling and quaking, yet pushing stoutly onward, straining her ears for some note of the brilliant stranger's.

It was mid-forenoon when she reached the region of the sumac, and as she hopped warily along, only a short distance from her, full and splendid, there burst the voice of the singer for whom she was searching. She sprang into air, and fled a mile before she realized that she was flying. Then she stopped and listened, and rolling with the river, she heard those bold true tones. Close to earth, she went back again, to see if, unobserved, she could find a spot where she might watch the stranger that had kissed her. When at last she reached a place where she could see him plainly, his beauty was so bewildering, and his song so enticing that she gradually hopped closer and closer without knowing she was moving.

High in the sumac the Cardinal had sung until his throat was parched, and the fountain of hope was almost dry. There was nothing save defeat from overwhelming numbers in Rainbow Bottom. He had paraded, and made all the music he ever had been taught, and improvised much more. Yet no one had come to seek him. Was it of necessity to be the Limberlost then? This one day more he would retain his dignity and his location. He tipped, tilted, and flirted. He whistled, and sang, and trilled. Over the lowland and up and down the shining river, ringing in every change he could invent, he sent for the last time his prophetic message, "Wet year! Wet year!"

"Come here! Come here!" entreated
the Cardinal

III

"Come here! Come here!" entreated the Cardinal

HE FELT that his music was not reaching his standard as he burst into this new song. He was almost discouraged. No way seemed open to him but flight to the Limberlost, and he so disdained the swamp that love-making would lose something of its greatest charm if he were driven there for a mate. The time seemed ripe for stringent measures, and the Cardinal was ready to take them; but how could he stringently urge a little mate that would not come on his imploring invitations? He listlessly pecked at the berries and flung abroad an inquiring "Chip!" With just an atom of hope, he

71

frequently mounted to his choir-loft and issued an order that savoured far more of a plea, "Come here! Come here!" and then, leaning, he listened intently to the voice of the river, lest he fail to catch the faintest responsive "Chook!" it might bear.

He could hear the sniffling of carp wallowing beside the bank. A big pickerel slashed around, breakfasting on minnows. Opposite the sumac, the black bass, with gamy spring, snapped up, before it struck the water, every luckless, honey-laden insect that fell from the feast of sweets in a blossom-whitened wild crab. The sharp bark of the red squirrel and the low of cattle, lazily chewing their cuds among the willows, came to him. The hammering of a woodpecker on a dead sycamore, a little above him, rolled to his straining ears like a drum beat.

The Cardinal hated the woodpecker more than he disliked the dove. It was only foolishly effusive, but the woodpecker was a veritable Bluebeard. The Cardinal longed to pull the feathers from his

back until it was as red as his head, for the woodpecker had dressed his suit in finest style, and with
dulcet tones and melting tenderness had gone
a-courting. Sweet as the dove's had been his wooing, and one more pang the lonely Cardinal had
suffered at being forced to witness his felicity; yet
scarcely had his plump, amiable little mate con-
sented to his caresses and approved the sycamore,
before he turned on her, pecked her severely, and
pulled a tuft of plumage from her breast. There
was not the least excuse for this tyrannical action;
and the sight filled the Cardinal with rage. He
fully expected to see Madam Woodpecker divorce
herself and flee her new home, and he most ear-
nestly hoped that she would; but she did no such
thing. She meekly flattened her feathers, hurried
work in a lively manner, and tried in every way to
anticipate and avert her mate's displeasure. Under
this treatment he grew more abusive, and now
Madam Woodpecker dodged every time she came
within his reach. It made the Cardinal feel so
vengeful that he longed to go up and drum the

sycamore with the woodpecker's head until he taught him how to treat his mate properly.

There was plently of lark music rolling with the river, and that morning brought the first liquid golden notes of the orioles. They had arrived at dawn, and were overjoyed with their homecoming, for they were darting from bank to bank singing exquisitely on wing. There seemed no end to the bird voices that floated with the river, and yet there was no beginning to the one voice for which the Cardinal waited with passionate longing.

The oriole's singing was so inspiring that it tempted the Cardinal to another effort, and perching where he gleamed crimson and black against the April sky, he tested his voice, and when sure of his tones, he entreatingly called: "Come here! Come here!"

Just then he saw her! She came daintily over the earth, soft as down before the wind, a rosy flush suffusing her plumage, a coral beak, her very feet pink—the shyest, most timid little thing alive.

Her bright eyes were popping with fear, and down there among the ferns, anemones and last year's dried leaves, she tilted her sleek crested head and peered at him with frightened wonder and silent helplessness.

It was for this the Cardinal had waited, hoped, and planned for many days. He had rehearsed what he conceived to be every point of the situation, and yet he was not prepared for the thing that suddenly happened to him. He had expected to reject many applicants before he selected one to match his charms; but instantly this shy little creature, slipping along near earth, taking a surreptitious peep at him, made him feel a very small bird, and he certainly never before had felt small. The crushing possibility that somewhere there might be a cardinal that was larger, brighter, and a finer musician than he, staggered him; and worst of all, his voice broke suddenly to his complete embarrassment.

Half screened by the flowers, she seemed so little, so shy, so delightfully sweet. He "chipped" carefully once or twice to steady himself and clear his throat, for unaccountably it had grown dry and husky; and then he tenderly tried again. "Come here! Come here!" implored the Cardinal. He forgot all about his dignity. He knew that his voice was trembling with eagerness and hoarse with fear. He was afraid to attempt approaching her, but he leaned toward her, begging and pleading. He teased and insisted, and he did not care a particle if he did. It suddenly seemed an honour to coax her. He rocked on the limb. He side-stepped and hopped and gyrated gracefully. He fluffed and flirted and showed himself to every advantage. It never occurred to him that the dove and the woodpecker might be watching, though he would not have cared in the least if they had been; and as for any other cardinal, he would have attacked the combined forces of the Limberlost and Rainbow Bottom.

He sang and sang. Every impulse of passion in his big, crimson, palpitating body was thrown into those notes; but she only turned her head from side to side, peering at him, seeming sufficiently frightened to flee at a breath, and answered not even the faintest little "Chook!" of encouragement.

The Cardinal rested a second before he tried again. That steadied him and gave him better command of himself. He could tell that his notes were clearing and growing sweeter. He was improving. Perhaps she was interested. There was some encouragement in the fact that she was still there. The Cardinal felt that his time had come.

"Come here! Come here!" He was on his mettle now. Surely no cardinal could sing fuller, clearer, sweeter notes! He began at the very first, and rollicked through a story of adventure, colouring it with every wild, dashing, catchy note he could improvise. He followed that with a rippling song of the joy and fulness of spring, in notes as light and airy as the wind-blown soul of melody, and with swaying body kept time to his rhythmic measures. Then he glided into a song of love, and tenderly, pleadingly, passionately, told the story as only a

77

courting bird can tell it. Then he sang a song of ravishment; a song quavering with fear and the pain tugging at his heart. He almost had run the gamut, and she really appeared as if she intended to flee rather than to come to him. He was afraid to take even one timid little hop toward her.

In a fit of desperation the Cardinal burst into the passion song. He arose to his full height, leaned toward her with outspread quivering wings, and crest flared to the utmost, and rocking from side to side in the intensity of his fervour, he poured out a perfect torrent of palpitant song. His cardinal body swayed to the rolling flood of his ecstatic tones, until he appeared like a flaming pulsing note of materialized music, as he entreated, coaxed, commanded, and pled. From sheer exhaustion, he threw up his head to round off the last note he could utter, and breathlessly glancing down to see if she were coming, caught sight of a faint streak of gray in the distance. He had planned so to subdue the little female he courted that she would come to him; he was in hot pursuit a half day's journey away before he remembered it.

No other cardinal ever endured such a chase as she led him in the following days. Through fear and timidity she had kept most of her life in the underbrush. The Cardinal was a bird of the open fields and tree-tops. He loved to rock with the wind, and speed arrow-like in great plunges of flight. This darting and twisting over logs, among leaves, and through tangled thickets, tired, tried, and exasperated him more than hundreds of miles of open flight. Sometimes he drove her from cover, and then she wildly dashed up-hill and down-dale, seeking another thicket; but wherever she went, the Cardinal was only a breath behind her, and with every passing mile his passion for her grew.

There was no time to eat, bathe, or sing; only mile after mile of unceasing pursuit. It seemed that the little creature could not stop if she would, and as for the Cardinal, he was in that chase to remain until his last heart-beat. It was a question how the frightened bird kept in advance. She was visibly the worse for this ardent courtship. Two tail feathers were gone, and there was a broken one beating from her wing. Once she had flown too low, striking her head against a rail until a drop of blood came, and she cried pitifully. Several times the Cardinal had cornered her, and tried to hold her by a bunch of feathers, and compel her by force to listen to reason; but she only broke from his hold and dashed away a stricken thing, leaving him half dead with longing and remorse.

But no matter how baffled she grew, or where she fled in her headlong flight, the one thing she always remembered, was not to lead the Cardinal into the punishment that awaited him in Rainbow Bottom. Panting for breath, quivering with fear, longing for well-concealed retreats, worn and half blinded by the disasters of flight through strange country, the tired bird beat her aimless way; but she would have been torn to pieces before she would have led her magnificent pursuer into the wrath of his enemies.

Poor little feathered creature! She had been flee-
ing some kind of danger all her life. She could not
realize that love and protection had come in this
splendid guise, and she fled on and on.

Once the Cardinal, aching with passion and
love, fell behind that she might rest, and before he
realized that another bird was close, an impudent
big relative of his, straying from the Limberlost,
entered the race and pursued her so hotly that
with a note of utter panic she wheeled and darted
back to the Cardinal for protection. When to the
rush of rage that possessed him at the sight of a
rival was added the knowledge that she was seeking him in her extremity, such a mighty wave of
anger swept the Cardinal that he appeared twice
his real size. Like a flaming brand of vengeance he
struck that Limberlost upstart, and sent him rolling to earth, a mass of battered feathers. With
beak and claw he made his attack, and when he so
utterly demolished his rival that he hopped away
trembling, with dishevelled plumage stained with
his own blood, the Cardinal remembered his little

81

love and hastened back, confidently hoping for his reward.

She was so securely hidden, that although he went searching, calling, pleading, he found no trace of her the remainder of that day. The Cardinal almost went distracted; and his tender imploring cries would have moved any except a panic-stricken bird. He did not even know in what direction to pursue her. Night closed down, and found him in a fever of love-sick fear, but it brought rest and wisdom. She could not have gone very far. She was too worn. He would not proclaim his presence. Soon she would suffer past enduring for food and water.

He hid in the willows close where he had lost her, and waited with what patience he could; and it was a wise plan. Shortly after dawn, moving stilly as the break of day, trembling with fear, she came slipping to the river for a drink. It was almost brutal cruelty, but her fear must be overcome someway; and with a cry of triumph the Cardinal, in a plunge of flight, was beside her. She gave him one stricken look, and dashed away. The chase began once more and continued until she was visibly breaking.

There was no room for a rival that morning. The Cardinal flew abreast of her and gave her a caress or attempted a kiss whenever he found the slightest chance. She was almost worn out, her flights were wavering and growing shorter. The Cardinal did his utmost. If she paused to rest, he crept close as he dared, and piteously begged: "Come here! Come here!"

When she took wing, he so dexterously intercepted her course that several time she found refuge in his sumac without realizing where she was. When she did that, he perched just as closely as he dared; and while they both rested, he sang to her a soft little whispered love song, deep in his throat; and with every note he gently edged nearer. She turned her head from him, and although she was panting for breath and palpitant with fear, the Cardinal knew that he dared not go closer, or she would dash away like the wild thing she was. The next time she took wing, she found him so persistently in her course that she turned sharply and fled panting to the sumac. When this had happened so often that she seemed to recognize the sumac as a place of refuge, the Cardinal slipped aside and spent all his remaining breath in an exultant whistle of triumph, for now he was beginning to see his way. He dashed into mid-air, and with a gyration that would have done credit to a flycatcher, he snapped up a gadfly that should have been more alert.

With a tender "Chip!" from branch to branch, slowly, cautiously, he came with it. Because he was half starved himself, he knew that she must be almost famished. Holding it where she could see, he hopped toward her, eagerly, carefully, the gadfly in his beak, his heart in his mouth. He stretched his neck and legs to the limit as he reached the fly toward her. What matter that she took it with a snap, and plunged a quarter of a mile before eating it? She had taken food from him! That was the beginning. Cautiously he impelled her toward the sumac, and with untiring patience kept her there the remainder of the day. He carried her every choice morsel he could find in the immediate vicinity of the sumac, and occasionally she took a bit from his beak, though oftenest he was compelled to lay it on a limb beside her. At dusk she repeatedly dashed toward the underbrush; but the Cardinal, with endless patience and tenderness, maneuvered her to the sumac, until she gave up, and beneath the shelter of a neighbouring grape-vine, perched on a limb that was the Cardinal's own chosen resting-place, tucked her tired head beneath her wing, and went to rest. When she was soundly sleeping, the Cardinal crept as closely as he dared, and with one eye on his little gray love, and the other roving for any possible danger, he spent a night of watching for any danger that might approach.

He was almost worn out; but this was infinitely better than the previous night, at any rate, for now he not only knew where she was, but she was fast asleep in his own favourite place. Huddled on the limb, the Cardinal gloated over her. He found her beauty perfect. To be sure, she was dishevelled; but she could make her toilet. There were a few feathers gone; but they would grow speedily. She made a heart-satisfying picture, on which the Cardinal feasted his love-sick soul, by the light of every straying moonbeam that slid around the edges of the grape leaves.

Wave after wave of tender passion shook him. In his throat half the night he kept softly calling to her: "Come here! Come here!"

Next morning, when the robins announced day beside the shining river, she awoke with a start; but before she could decide in which direction to fly, she discovered a nice fresh grub laid on the limb close to her, and very sensibly remained for breakfast. Then the Cardinal went to the river and bathed. He made such delightful play of it, and the splash of the water sounded so refreshing to the tired draggled bird, that she could not resist venturing for a few dips. When she was wet she could not fly well, and he improved the opportunity to pull her broken quills, help her dress herself, and bestow a few extra caresses. He guided her to his favourite place for a sun bath; and followed the farmer's plow in the corn field until he found a big sweet beetle. He snapped off its head, peeled the stiff wing shields, and daintily offered it to her. He was so delighted when she took it from his beak, and remained in the sumac to eat it, that he established himself on an adjoining thorn-bush, where the snowy blossoms of a wild morning-glory made a fine background for his scarlet coat. He sang the old pleading song as he never had sung it before, for now there was a tinge of hope battling with the fear in his heart.

Over and over he sang, rounding, fulling, swelling every note, leaning toward her in coaxing tenderness, flashing his brilliant beauty as he swayed and rocked, for her approval; and all that he had suffered and all that he hoped for was in his song. Just when his heart was growing sick within him, his straining ear caught the faintest, most timid call a lover ever answered. Only one imploring, gentle "Chook!" from the sumac! His song broke in a suffocating burst of exultation. Cautiously he hopped from twig to twig toward her. With tender throaty murmurings he slowly edged nearer, and wonder of wonders! with tired eyes and quivering wings, she reached him her beak for a kiss.

At dinner that day, the farmer said to his wife:

"Maria, if you want to hear the prettiest singin', an' see the cutest sight you ever saw, jest come down along the line fence an' watch the antics o' that redbird we been hearin'."

"I don't know as redbirds are so scarce 'at I've any call to wade through slush a half-mile to see one," answered Maria.

"Footin's pretty good along the line fence," said Abram, "an' you never saw a redbird like this fellow. He's as big as any two common ones. He's so red every bush he lights on looks like it was afire. It's past all question, he's been somebody's pet, an' he's taken me for the man. I can get in six feet of him easy. He's the finest bird I ever set eyes on; an'

88

as for singin', he's dropped the weather, an' he's askin' folks to his housewarmin' to-day. He's been there alone for a week, an' his singin's been first-class; but to-day he's picked up a mate, an' he's as tickled as ever I was. I am really consarned for fear he'll burst himself."

Maria sniffed.

"Course, don't come if you're tired, honey," said the farmer. "I thought maybe you'd enjoy it. He's a-doin' me a power o' good. My joints are limbered up till I catch myself pretty near runnin', on the up furrow, an' then, down towards the fence, I go slow so's to stay near him as long as I can."

Maria stared. "Abram Johnson, have you gone daft?" she demanded.

Abram chuckled. "Not a mite dafter'n you'll be, honey, once you set eyes on the fellow. Better come, if you can. You're invited. He's askin' the whole endurin' country to come."

Maria said nothing more; but she mentally decided she had no time to fool with a bird, when there were housekeeping and spring sewing to do. As she recalled Abram's enthusiastic praise of the singer, and had a whiff of the odour-laden air as she passed from kitchen to spring-house, she was compelled to admit that it was a temptation to go; but she finished her noon work and resolutely sat down with her needle. She stitched industriously, her thread straightening with a quick nervous sweep, learned through years of experience; and if her eyes wandered riverward, and if she paused frequently with arrested hand and listened intently, she did not realize it. By two o'clock, a spirit of unrest that demanded recognition had taken possession of her. Setting her lips firmly, a scowl clouding her brow, she stitched on. By half past two her hands dropped in her lap, Abram's new hickory shirt slid to the floor, and she hesitatingly arose and crossed the room to the closet, from which she took her overshoes, and set them by the kitchen fire, to have them ready in case she wanted them.

"Pshaw!" she muttered, "I got this shirt to finish this afternoon. There's butter an' bakin' in the mornin', an' Mary Jane Simms is comin' for a visit in the afternoon."

She returned to the window and took up the shirt, sewing with unusual swiftness for the next half-hour; but by three she dropped it, and opening the kitchen door, gazed toward the river.

Every intoxicating delight of early spring was in the air. The breeze that fanned her cheek was laden with subtle perfume of pollen and the crisp fresh odour of unfolding leaves. Curling skyward, like a beckoning finger, went a spiral of violet and gray smoke from the log heap Abram was burning; and scattered over spaces of a mile were half a dozen others, telling a story of the activity of his neighbours. Like the low murmur of distant music came the beating wings of hundreds of her bees, rimming the water trough, insane with thirst. On the wood-pile the guinea cock clattered incessantly: "Phut rack! Phut rack!" Across the dooryard came the old turkey-gobbler with fan tail and a rasping scrape of wing, evincing his delight in spring and mating time by a series of explosive snorts. On the barnyard gate the old Shanghai was lustily challenging to mortal combat one of his kind three miles across country. From the river the river arose the strident scream of her blue gander jealously guarding his harem. In the poultry-yard the hens made a noisy cackling party, and the stable lot was filled with cattle bellowing for the freedom of the meadow pasture, as yet scarcely ready for grazing. It seemed to the little woman, hesitating in the doorway, as if all nature had entered into a conspiracy to lure her from her work, and just then, clear and imperious, arose the demand of the Cardinal: "Come here! Come here!"

Blank amazement filled her face. "As I'm a livin' woman!" she gasped. "He's changed his song! That's what Abram meant by me bein' invited. He's askin' folks to see his mate. I'm goin'."

The dull red of excitement sprang into her cheeks. She hurried on her overshoes, and drew an old shawl over her head. She crossed the dooryard, followed the path through the orchard, and came to the lane. Below the barn she turned back and attempted to cross. The mud was deep and thick, and she lost an overshoe; but with the help of a stick she pried it out, and replaced it.

"Joke on me if I'd a-tumbled over in this mud," she muttered.

She entered the barn, and came out a minute later, carefully closing and buttoning the door, and started down the line fence toward the river.

Half-way across the field Abram saw her coming. No need to recount how often he had looked in that direction during the afternoon. He slapped the lines on the old gray's back and came tearing down the slope, his eyes flashing, his cheeks red, his hands firmly gripping the plow that rolled up a line of black mould as he passed.

Maria, staring at his flushed face and shining eyes, recognized that his whole being proclaimed an inward exultation.

"Abram Johnson," she solemnly demanded, "have you got the power?"

"Yes," cried Abram, pulling off his old felt hat,

93

and gazing into the crown as if for inspiration. "You've said it, honey! I got the power! Got it of a little red bird! Power o' spring! Power o' song! Power o' love! If that poor little red target for some ornery cuss's bullet can get all he's getting out o' life to-day, there's no cause why a reasonin' thinkin' man shouldn't realize some o' his blessings. You hit it, Maria; I got the power. It's the power o' God, but I learned how to lay hold of it from that little red bird. Come here, Maria!"

Abram wrapped the lines around the plow handle, and cautiously led his wife to the fence. He found a piece of thick bark for her to stand on, and placed her where she would be screened by a big oak. Then he stood behind her and pointed out the sumac and the female bird.

"Jest you keep still a minute, an' you'll feel paid for comin' all right, honey," he whispered, "but don't make any sudden movement."

"I don't know as I ever saw a worse-lookin' specimen 'an she is," answered Maria.

"She looks first-class to him. There's no kick

comin' on his part, I can tell you," replied Abram.

The bride hopped shyly through the sumac. She pecked at the dried berries, and frequently tried to improve her plumage, which certainly had been badly draggled; and there was a drop of blood dried at the base of her beak. She plainly showed the effects of her rough experience, and yet she was a most attractive bird; for the dimples in her plump body showed through the feathers, and instead of the usual wickedly black eyes of the cardinal family, hers were a soft tender brown touched by a love-light there was no mistaking. She was a beautiful bird, and she was doing all in her power to make herself dainty again. Her movements clearly indicated how timid she was, and yet she remained in the sumac as if she feared to leave it; and frequently peered expectantly among the tree-tops.

There was a burst of exultation down the river. The little bird gave her plumage a fluff, and watched anxiously. On came the Cardinal like a flaming rocket, calling to her on wing. He alighted

95

beside her, dropped into her beak a morsel of food, gave her a kiss to aid digestion, caressingly ran his beak the length of her wing quills, and flew to the dogwood. Mrs. Cardinal enjoyed the meal. It struck her palate exactly right. She liked the kiss and caress, cared, in fact, for all that he did for her, and with the appreciation of his tenderness came repentance for the dreadful chase she had led him in her foolish fright, and an impulse to repay. She took a dainty hop toward the dogwood, and the invitation she sent him was exquisite. With a shrill whistle of exultant triumph the Cardinal answered at a headlong rush.

The farmer's grip tightened on his wife's shoulder, but Maria turned toward him with blazing, tear-filled eyes. "An' you call yourself a decent man, Abram Johnson?"

"Decent?" quavered the astonished Abram. "Decent? I believe I am."

"I believe you ain't," hotly retorted his wife. "You don't know what decency is, if you go peekin' at them. They ain't birds! They're folks!"

"Maria," pled Abram, "Maria, honey."

"I am plumb ashamed of you," broke in Maria. "How d'you s'pose she'd feel if she knew there was a man here peekin' at her? Ain't she got a right to be lovin' and tender? Ain't she got a right to pay him best she knows? They're jest common human bein's, an' I don't know where you got privilege to spy on a female when she's doin' the best she knows."

Maria broke from his grasp and started down the line fence.

In a few strides Abram had her in his arms, his withered cheek with its springtime bloom pressed against her equally withered, tear-stained one.

"Maria," he whispered, waveringly, "Maria, honey, I wasn't meanin' any disrespect to the sex."

Maria wiped her eyes on the corner of her shawl. "I don't s'pose you was, Abram," she admitted; "but you're jest like all the rest o' the men. You never think! Now you go on with your plowin' an' let that little female alone."

97

She unclasped his arms and turned homeward.

"Honey," called Abram softly, "since you brought 'em that pocketful o' wheat, you might as well let me have it."

"Landy!" exclaimed Maria, blushing; "I plumb forgot my wheat! I thought maybe, bein' so early, pickin' was scarce, an' if you'd put out a little wheat an' a few crumbs, they'd stay an' nest in the sumac, as you're so fond o' them."

"Jest what I'm fairly prayin' they'll do, an' I been carryin' stuff an' pettin' him up best I knowed for a week," said Abram, as he knelt, and cupped his shrunken hands, while Maria guided the wheat from her apron into them. "I'll scatter it along the top rail, an' they'll be after it in fifteen minutes. Thank you, Maria. 'Twas good o' you to think of it."

Maria watched him steadily. How dear he was! How dear he always had been! How happy they were together! "Abram," she asked, hesitatingly, "is there anything else I could do for—your birds?"

They were creatures of habitual repression, and

the inner glimpses they had taken of each other that day were surprises they scarcely knew how to meet. Abram said nothing, because he could not. He slowly shook his head, and turned to the plow, his eyes misty. Maria started toward the line fence, but she paused repeatedly to listen; and it was no wonder, for all the redbirds from miles down the river had gathered around the sumac to see if there were a battle in birdland; but it was only the Cardinal, turning somersaults in the air, and screaming with bursting exuberance: "Come here! Come here!"

"So dear! So dear!" crooned the Cardinal

IV

"So dear! So dear!" crooned the Cardinal!

SHE had taken possession of the sumac. The location was her selection and he loudly applauded her
choice. She placed the first twig, and after ex-
amining it carefully, he spent the day carrying her
others just as much like it as possible. If she used
a dried grass blade, he carried grass blades until
she began dropping them on the ground. If she
worked in a bit of wild grape-vine bark, he peeled
grape-vines until she would have no more. It never
occurred to him that he was the largest cardinal
in the woods, in those days, and he had forgotten
that he wore a red coat. She was not a skilled archi-

tect. Her nest certainly was a loose ramshackle affair; but she had built it, and had allowed him to help her. It was hers; and he improvised a pæan in its praise. Every morning he perched on the edge of the nest and gazed in songless wonder at each beautiful new egg; and whenever she came to brood she sat as if entranced, eyeing her treasures in an ecstasy of proud possession.

Then she nestled them against her warm breast, and turned adoring eyes toward the Cardinal. If he sang from the dogwood, she faced that way. If he rocked on the wild grape-vine, she turned in her nest. If he went to the corn field for grubs, she stood astride her eggs and peered down, watching his every movement with unconcealed anxiety. The Cardinal forgot to be vain of his beauty; she delighted in it every hour of the day. Shy and timid beyond belief she had been during her courtship; but she made reparation by being an incomparably generous and devoted mate.

And the Cardinal! He was astonished to find himself capable of so much and such varied feeling. It was not enough that he brooded while she went to bathe and exercise. The daintiest of every morsel he found was carried to her. When she refused to swallow another particle, he perched on a twig close by the nest many times in a day; and with sleek feathers and lowered crest, gazed at her in silent worshipful adoration.

Up and down the river bank he flamed and rioted. In the sumac he uttered not the faintest "Chip!" that might attract attention. He was so anxious to be inconspicuous that he appeared only half his real size. Always on leaving he gave her a tender little peck and ran his beak the length of her wing—a characteristic caress that he delighted to bestow on her.

If he felt that he was disturbing her too often, he perched on the dogwood and sang for life, and love, and happiness. His music was in a minor key now. The high, exultant, ringing notes of passion were mellowed and subdued. He was improvising cradle songs and lullabies. He was telling her how he loved her, how he would fight for her, how he was watching over her, how he would signal if any danger were approaching, how proud he was of her, what a perfect nest she had built, how beautiful he thought her eggs, what magnificent babies they would produce. Full of tenderness, melting with love, liquid with sweetness, the Cardinal sang to his patient little brooding mate: "So dear! So dear!"

The farmer leaned on his corn-planter and listened to him intently. "I swanny! If he hasn't changed his song again, an' this time I'm blest if I can tell what he's saying!" Every time the Cardinal lifted his voice, the clip of the corn-planter ceased, and Abram hung on the notes and studied them over.

One night he said to his wife: "Maria, have you been noticin' the redbird of late? He's changed to a new tune, an' this time I'm completely stalled. I can't for the life of me make out what he's saying. S'pose you step down to-morrow an' see if you can catch it for me. I'd give a pretty to know!"

Maria felt flattered. She always had believed

that she had a musical ear. Here was an opportunity to test it and please Abram at the same time. She hastened her work the following morning, and very early slipped along the line fence. Hiding behind the oak, with straining ear and throbbing heart, she eagerly listened. "Clip, clip," came the sound of the planter, as Abram's dear old figure trudged up the hill. "Chip! Chip!" came the warning of the Cardinal, as he flew to his mate.

He gave her some food, stroked her wing, and flying to the dogwood, sang of the love that encompassed him. As he trilled forth his tender caressing strain, the heart of the listening woman translated as did that of the brooding bird.

With shining eyes and flushed cheeks, she sped down the fence. Panting and palpitating with excitement, she met Abram half-way on his return trip. Forgetful of her habitual reserve, she threw her arms around his neck, and drawing his face to hers, she cried: "Oh, Abram! I got it! I got it! I know what he's saying! Oh, Abram, my love! My own! To me so dear! So dear!"

"So dear! So dear!" echoed the Cardinal.

The bewilderment in Abram's face melted into comprehension. He swept Maria from her feet as he lifted his head.

"On my soul! You have got it, honey! That's what he's saying, plain as gospel! I can tell it plainer'n anything he's sung yet, now I sense it."

He gathered Maria in his arms, pressed her head against his breast with a trembling old hand, while the face he turned to the morning was beautiful.

"I wish to God," he said quaveringly, " 'at every creature on earth was as well fixed as me an' the redbird!" Clasping each other, they listened with rapt faces, as, mellowing across the corn field, came the notes of the Cardinal: "So dear! So dear!"

After that Abram's devotion to his bird family became a mild mania. He carried food to the top rail of the line fence every day, rain or shine, with the same regularity that he curried and fed Nancy in the barn. From caring for and so loving the Cardinal, there grew in his tender old heart a

welling flood of sympathy for every bird that
homed on his farm.

He drove a stake to mark the spot where the
killdeer hen brooded in the corn field, so that he
would not drive Nancy over the nest. When he
closed the bars at the end of the lane, he always
was careful to leave the third one down, for there
was a chippy brooding in the opening where it
fitted when closed. Alders and sweetbriers grew
in his fence corners undisturbed that spring if he
discovered that they sheltered an anxious-eyed little mother. He left a square yard of clover un-
mowed, because it seemed to him that the lark,
singing nearer the Throne than any other bird,
was picking up stray notes dropped by the In-
visible Choir, and with unequalled purity and
tenderness, sending them ringing down to his
brooding mate, whose home and happiness would
be despoiled by the reaping of that spot of green.
He delayed burning the brush-heap from the
spring pruning, back of the orchard, until fall,
when he found it housed a pair of fine thrushes;

for the song of the thrush delighted him almost as much as that of the lark. He left a hollow limb on the old red pearmain apple-tree, because when he came to cut it there was a pair of bluebirds twittering around, frantic with anxiety.

His pockets were bulgy with wheat and crumbs, and his heart was big with happiness. It was the golden springtime of his later life. The sky never had seemed so blue, or the earth so beautiful. The Cardinal had opened the fountains of his soul; life took on a new colour and joy; while every work of God manifested a fresh and heretofore unappreciated loveliness. His very muscles seemed to relax, and new strength arose to meet the demands of his uplifted spirit. He had not finished his day's work with such ease and pleasure in years; and he could see the influence of his rejuvenation in Maria. She was flitting around her house with broken snatches of song, even sweeter to Abram's ears than the notes of the birds; and in recent days he had noticed that she dressed particularly for her afternoon's sewing, putting on her Sunday lace collar and a white apron. He immediately went to town and bought her a finer collar than she ever had owned in her life.

Then he hunted a sign painter, and came home bearing a number of pine boards on which gleamed in big, shiny black letters:

```
NO  HUNTING  ALLOWED
ON  THIS  FARM
```

He seemed slightly embarrassed when he showed them to Maria. "I feel a little mite on-friendly, putting up signs like that 'fore my neighbours," he admitted, "but the fact is, it ain't the neighbours so much as it's boys that need raising, an' them town creatures who call themselves sportsmen, an' kill a hummin'-bird to see if they can hit it. Time was when trees an' underbrush were full o' birds an' squirrels, any amount o' rabbits, an' the fish fairly crowdin' in the river. I used to kill all the quail an' wild turkeys about here

111

a body needed to make an appetizing change. It was always my plan to take a little an' leave a little. But jest look at it now. Surprise o' my life if I get a two-pound bass. Wild turkey gobblin' would scare me most out of my senses, an', as for the birds, there are jest about a fourth what there used to be, an' the crops eaten to pay for it. I'd do all I'm tryin' to for any bird, because of its song an' colour, an' pretty teeterin' ways, but I ain't so slow but I see I'm paid in what they do for me. Up go these signs, an' it won't be a happy day for anybody I catch trespassin' on my birds."

Maria studied the signs meditatively. "You shouldn't be forced to put 'em up," she said conclusively. "If it's been decided 'at it's good for 'em to be here, an' laws made to protect 'em, people ought to act with some sense, an' leave them alone. I never was so int'rested in the birds in all my life; an' I'll jest do a little lookin' out myself. If you hear a spang o' the dinner bell when you're out in the field, you'll know it means there's some one sneakin' 'round with a gun."

Abram caught Maria, and planted a resounding smack on her cheek, where the roses of girlhood yet bloomed for him. Then he filled his pockets with crumbs and grain, and strolled to the river to set the Cardinal's table. He could hear the sharp incisive "Chip!" and the tender mellow love-notes as he left the barn; and all the way to the sumac they rang in his ears.

The Cardinal met him at the corner of the field, and hopped over bushes and the fence only a few yards from him. When Abram had scattered his store on the rail, the bird came tipping and tilting, daintily caught up a crumb, and carried it to the sumac. His mate was pleased to take it; and he carried her one morsel after another until she refused to open her beak for more. He made a light supper himself; and then swinging on the grape-vine, he closed the day with an hour of music. He repeatedly turned a bright questioning eye toward Abram, but he never for a moment lost sight of the nest and the plump gray figure of his little mate. As she brooded over her eggs, he brooded over her; and that she might realize the depth and constancy of his devotion, he told her repeatedly, with every tender inflection he could throw into his tones, that she was "So dear! So dear!"

The Cardinal had not known that the coming of the mate he so coveted would fill his life with such unceasing gladness, and yet, on the very day that happiness seemed at fullest measure, there was trouble in the sumac. He had overstayed his time, chasing a fat moth he particularly wanted for his mate, and she, growing thirsty past endurance, left the nest and went to the river. Seeing her there, he made all possible haste to take his turn at brooding, so he arrived just in time to see a pilfering red squirrel starting away with an egg.

With a vicious scream the Cardinal struck him full force. His rush of rage cost the squirrel an eye; but it lost the father a birdling, for the squirrel dropped the egg outside the nest. The Cardinal mournfully carried away the tell-tale bits of shell, so that any one seeing them would not look up and discover his treasures. That left three eggs; and the brooding bird mourned over the lost one so pitifully that the Cardinal perched close to the nest the remainder of the day, and whispered over and over for her comfort that she was "So dear! So dear!"

"See here! See here!" demanded
the Cardinal

V

"See here! See here!" demanded
the Cardinal

THE mandate repeatedly rang from the topmost
twig of the thorn tree, and yet the Cardinal was
not in earnest. He was beside himself with a new
and delightful excitement, and he found it im-
possible to refrain from giving vent to his feelings.
He was commanding the farmer and every furred
and feathered denizen of the river bottom to see;
then he fought like a wild thing if any of them
ventured close, for great things were happening
in the sumac.

In past days the Cardinal had brooded an hour
every morning while his mate went to take her

exercise, bathe, and fluff in the sun parlour. He had gone to her that morning as usual, and she looked at him with anxious eyes and refused to move. He had hopped to the very edge of the nest and repeatedly urged her to go. She only ruffled her feathers, and nestled the eggs she was brooding to turn them, but did not offer to leave. The Cardinal reached over and gently nudged her with his beak, to remind her that it was his time to brood; but she looked at him almost savagely, and gave him a sharp peck; so he knew she was not to be bothered. He carried her every dainty he could find and hovered near her, tense with anxiety.

It was late in the afternoon before she went after the drink for which she was half famished. She scarcely had reached a willow and bent over the water before the Cardinal was on the edge of the nest. He examined it closely, but he could see no change. He leaned to give the eggs careful scrutiny, and from somewhere there came to him the faintest little "Chip!" he ever had heard. Up went the Cardinal's crest, and he dashed to the willow.

There was no danger in sight; and his mate was greedily dipping her rosy beak in the water. He went back to the cradle and listened intently, and again that feeble cry came to him. Under the nest, around it, and all through the sumac he searched, until at last, completely baffled, he came back to the edge. The sound was so much plainer there, that he suddenly leaned, caressing the eggs with his beak; then the Cardinal knew! He had heard the first faint cries of his shell-incased babies!

With a wild scream he made a flying leap through the air. His heart was beating to suffocation. He started in a race down the river. If he alighted on a bush he took only one swing, and springing from it flamed on in headlong flight. He flashed to the top of the tallest tulip tree, and cried cloudward to the lark: "See here! See here!" He dashed to the river bank and told the killdeers, and then visited the underbrush and informed the thrushes and wood robins. Father-tender, he grew so delirious with joy that he forgot his habitual aloofness, and fraternized with every bird beside the shining river. He even laid aside his customary caution, went chipping into the sumac, and caressed his mate so boisterously she gazed at him severely and gave his wing a savage pull to recall him to his sober senses.

That night the Cardinal slept in the sumac, very close to his mate, and he shut only one eye at a time. Early in the morning, when he carried her the first food, he found that she was on the edge of the nest, dropping bits of shell outside; and creeping to peep, he saw the tiniest coral baby, with closed eyes, and little patches of soft silky down. Its beak was wide open, and though his heart was even fuller than on the previous day, the Cardinal knew what that meant; and instead of indulging in another celebration, he assumed the duties of paternity, and began searching for food, for now there were two empty crops in his family. On the following day there were four. Then he really worked. How eagerly he searched, and how gladly he flew to the sumac with every rare morsel! The babies were too small for the mother to leave; and for the first few days the Cardinal was constantly on wing.

If he could not find sufficiently dainty food for them in the trees and bushes, or among the offerings of the farmer, he descended to earth and searched like a wood robin. He forgot he needed a bath or owned a sun parlour; but everywhere he went, from his full heart there constantly burst the cry:

"See here! See here!"

His mate made never a sound. Her eyes were bigger and softer than ever, and in them glowed a steady lovelight. She hovered over those three red mites of nestlings so tenderly! She was so absorbed in feeding, stroking, and coddling them she neglected herself until she became quite lean. When the Cardinal came every few minutes with food, she was a picture of love and gratitude for his devoted attention, and once she reached over and softly kissed his wing. "See here! See here!" shrilled the Cardinal; and in his ecstasy he again forgot himself and sang in the sumac. Then he carried food with greater activity than ever to cover his lapse.

The farmer knew that it lacked an hour of noon, but he was so anxious to tell Maria the news that he could not endure the suspense another minute. There was a new song from the sumac. He had heard it as he turned the first corner with the shovel plow. He had listened eagerly, and had caught the meaning almost at once—"See here! See here!" He tied the old gray mare to the fence to prevent her eating the young corn, and went immediately. By leaning a rail against the thorn tree he was able to peer into the sumac, and take a good look at the nest of handsome birdlings, now well screened with the umbrella-like foliage. It seemed to Abram that he never could wait until noon. He critically examined the harness, in the hope that he would find a buckle missing, and tried to discover a flaw in the plow that would send him to the barn for a file; but he could not invent an excuse for going. So, when he had waited until an hour of noon, he could endure it no longer.

"Got news for you, Maria," he called from the well, where he was making a pretense of thirst.

"Oh I don't know," answered Maria, with a superior smile. "If it's about the redbirds, he's been up to the garden three times this morning yellin', 'See here!' fit to split; an' I jest figured that their little ones had hatched. Is that your news?"

"Well I be durned!" gasped the astonished Abram.

Mid-afternoon Abram turned Nancy and started the plow down a row that led straight to the sumac. He intended to stop there, tie to the fence, and go to the river bank, in the shade, for a visit with the Cardinal. It was very warm, and he was feeling the heat so much, that in his heart he knew he would be glad to reach the end of the row and the rest he had promised himself.

The quick nervous strokes of the dinner bell, "Clang! Clang!" came cutting the air clearly and sharply. Abram stopped Nancy with a jerk. It was the warning Maria had promised to send him if she saw prowlers with guns. He shaded his eyes with his hand and scanned the points of the compass through narrowed lids with concentrated vision. He first caught a gleam of light playing on a gun-barrel, and then he could discern the figure of a man clad in hunter's outfit leisurely walking down the lane, toward the river.

Abram hastily hitched Nancy to the fence. By making the best time he could, he reached the opposite corner, and was nibbling the midrib of a young corn blade and placidly viewing the landscape when the hunter passed.

"Howdy!" he said in an even cordial voice.

The hunter walked on without lifting his eyes or making audible reply. To Abram's friendly old-fashioned heart this seemed the rankest discourtesy; and there was a flash in his eye and a certain quality in his voice he lifted a hand for parley.

"Hold a minute, my friend," he said. "Since you are on my premises, might I be privileged to ask if you have seen a few signs 'at I have posted pertainin' to the use of a gun?"

"I am not blind," replied the hunter; "and my education has been looked after to the extent that I can make out your notices. From the number and size of them, I think I could do it, old man, if I had no eyes."

The scarcely suppressed sneer, and the "old man" grated on Abram's nerves amazingly, for a man of sixty years of peace. The gleam in his eyes grew stronger, and there was a perceptible lift of his shoulders as he answered:

"I meant 'em to be read an' understood! From the main road passin' that cabin up there on the bank, straight to the river, an' from the furthermost line o' this field to the same, is my premises, an' on every foot of 'em the signs are in full force. They're in a little fuller force in June, when half the bushes an' tufts o' grass are housin' a young bird family, 'an at any other time. They're sort o' upholdin' the legislature's act, providing for the protection o' game an' singin' birds; an' maybe it 'ud be well for you to notice 'at I'm not so old but I'm able to stand up for my right to any livin' man."

There certainly was an added tinge of respect in the hunter's tones as he asked: "Would you consider it trespass if a man simply crossed your land, following the line of the fences to reach the farm of a friend?"

"Certainly not!" cried Abram, cordial in his relief. "To be sure not! Glad to have you convenience yourself. I only wanted to jest call to your notice 'at the *birds* are protected on this farm."

"I have no intention of interfering with your precious birds, I assure you," replied the hunter. "And if you require an explanation of the gun in June, I confess I did hope to be able to pick off a squirrel for a very sick friend. But I suppose for even such cause it would not be allowed on your premises."

"Oh pshaw now!" said Abram. "Man alive! I'm not onreasonable. O' course in case o' sickness I'd be glad if you could run across a squirrel. All I wanted was to have a clear understandin' about the birds. Good luck, an' good day to you!"

Abram started across the field to Nancy, but he

repeatedly turned to watch the gleam of the gun-barrel, as the hunter rounded the corner and started down the river bank. He saw him leave the line of the fence and disappear in the thicket.

"Goin' straight for the sumac," muttered Abram. "It's likely I'm a fool for not stayin' right beside him past that point. An' yet—I made it fair an' plain, an' he passed his word 'at he wouldn't touch the birds."

He untied Nancy, and for the second time started toward the sumac. He had been plowing carefully, his attention divided between the mare and the corn; but he uprooted half that row, for his eyes wandered to the Cardinal's home as if he were fascinated, and his hands were shaking with undue excitement as he gripped the plow handles. At last he stopped Nancy, and stood gazing eagerly toward the river.

"Must be jest about the sumac," he whispered. "Lord! but I'll be glad to see the old gun-barrel gleamin' safe t'other side o' it."

There was a thin puff of smoke, and a screaming

echo went rolling and reverberating down the Wabash. Abram's eyes widened, and a curious whiteness settled on his lips. He stood as if incapable of moving. "Clang! Clang!" came Maria's second warning.

The trembling slid from him, and his muscles hardened. There was no trace of rheumatic stiffness in his movements. With a bound he struck the chain-traces from the singletree at Nancy's heels. He caught the hames, leaped on her back, and digging his heels into her sides, he stretched along her neck like an Indian and raced across the corn field. Nancy's twenty years slipped from her as her master's sixty had from him. Without understanding the emergency, she knew that he required all the speed there was in her; and with trace-chains rattling and beating on her heels, she stretched out until she fairly swept the young corn, as she raced for the sumac. Once Abram straightened, and slipping a hand into his pocket, drew out a formidable jack-knife, opening it as he rode. When he reached the fence, he almost flew over Nancy's head. He went into a fence corner, and with a few slashes severed a stout hickory withe, stripping the leaves and topping it as he leaped the fence.

He grasped this ugly weapon, his eyes dark with anger as he appeared before the hunter, who supposed him at the other side of the field.

"Did you shoot at that redbird?" he roared.

As his gun was at the sportman's shoulder, and he was still peering among the bushes, denial seemed useless. "Yes, I did," he replied, and made a pretense of turning to the sumac again.

There was a forward impulse of Abram's body. "Hit 'im?" he demanded with awful calm.

"Thought I had, but I guess I only winged him."

Abram's fingers closed around his club. At the sound of his friend's voice, the Cardinal came darting through the bushes a wavering flame, and swept so closely to him for protection that a wing almost brushed his cheek.

"See here! See here!" shrilled the bird in deadly panic. There was not a cut feather on him.

Abram's relief was so great he seemed to shrink an inch in height.

"Young man, you better thank your God you missed that bird," he said solemnly, "for if you'd killed him, I'd a-mauled this stick to ribbons on you, an' I'm most afraid I wouldn't a-knowed when to quit."

He advanced a step in his eagerness, and the hunter, mistaking his motive, levelled his gun.

"Drop that!" shouted Abram, as he broke through the bushes that clung to him, tore the clothing from his shoulders, and held him back. "Drop that! Don't you dare point a weapon at me; on my own premises, an' after you passed your word.

"Your word!" repeated Abram, with withering scorn, his white, quivering old face terrible to see. "Young man, I got a couple o' things to say to you. You'r' shaped like a man, an' you'r' dressed like a man, an' yet the smartest person livin' would never take you for anything but an egg-suckin' dog, this minute. All the time God ever spent on you was wasted, an' your mother's had the same luck. I s'pose God's used to having creatures 'at He's made go wrong, but I pity your mother. Goodness knows a woman suffers an' works enough over her children, an' then to fetch a boy to man's estate an' have him, of his own free will an' accord, be a liar! Young man, truth is the cornerstone o' the temple o' character. Nobody can put up a good buildin' without a solid foundation; an' you can't do solid character buildin' with a lie at the base. Man 'at's a liar ain't fit for anything! Can't trust him in no sphere or relation o' life; or in any way, shape, or manner. You passed out your word like a man, an' like a man I took it an' went off trustin' you, an' you failed me. Like as not that squirrel story was a lie, too! Have you got a sick friend who is needin' squirrel broth?"

The hunter shook his head.

"No? That wasn't true either? I'll own you make me curious. 'Ud you mind tellin' me what was your idy in cookin' up that squirrel story?"

The hunter spoke with an effort. "I suppose I

wanted to do something to make you feel small," he admitted, in a husky voice.

"You wanted to make me feel small," repeated Abram, wonderingly. "Lord! Lord! Young man, did you ever hear o' a boomerang? It's a kind o' weapon used in Borneo, er Australy, er some o' them furrin parts, an' it's so made 'at the heathens can pitch it, an' it cuts a circle an' comes back to the fellow 'at throwed. I can't see myself, an' I don't know how small I'm lookin'; but I'd rather lose ten year o' my life 'an to have anybody catch me lookin' as little as you do right now. I guess we look about the way we feel in this world. I'm feelin' near the size o' Goliath at present; but your size is such 'at it hustles me to see any *man* in you at all. An' you wanted to make me feel small! My, oh, my! An' you so young yet, too!

"An' if it hadn't a-compassed a matter o' breakin' your word, what 'ud you want to kill the redbird for, anyhow? Who give you rights to go 'round takin' such beauty an' joy out of the world? Who do you think made this world an' the things 'at's in it? Maybe it's your notion 'at somebody about your size whittled it from a block o' wood, scattered a little sand for earth, stuck a few seeds for trees, an' started the oceans with a waterin'-pot! I don't know what paved streets an' stall feedin' do for a man, but any one 'at's lived sixty year on the ground knows 'at this whole old earth is jest teemin' with work 'at's too big for anything but a God, an' a mighty *big* God at that!

"You don't never need bother none 'bout the diskivries o' science, for if science could prove 'at the earth was a red hot slag broken from the sun, 'at balled an' cooled flyin' through space until the force o' gravity caught an' held it, it doesn't prove what the sun broke from, or why it balled an' didn't cool. Sky over your head, earth under foot, trees around you, an' river there—all full o' life 'at you ain't no mortal right to touch, 'cos God made it, an' it's His! Course, I know 'at He said distinct 'at man was to have 'dominion over the beasts o' the field, an' the fowls o' the air.' An' that means 'at you're free to smash a copperhead instead of letting it sting you. Means 'at you better shoot a wolf than to let it carry off your lambs. Means 'at it's right to kill a hawk an' save your chickens; but God knows 'at shootin' a redbird just to see the feathers fly isn't having dominion over anything; it's jest makin' a plumb beast o' *yerself*. Passes me, how you can face up to the Almighty, an' draw a bead on a thing like that! Takes more gall'n I got!

"God never made anything prettier 'an that bird, an' He must a-been mighty proud o' the job. Jest cast your eyes on it there! Ever see anything so runnin' over with dainty, pretty, coaxin' ways? Little red creatures, full o' hist'ry, too! Ever think o' that? Last year's bird, hatched hereabout, like as not. Went South for winter, an' made friends 'at's been feedin', an' teachin' it to *trust* mankind. Back this spring in a night, an' struck that sumac over a month ago. Broke me all up first time I ever set eyes on it.

"Biggest reddest redbird I ever saw; an' jest a master hand at king's English! Talk plain as you can! Don't know what he said down South, but you can bank on it, it was sumpin' pretty fine. When he settled here, he was discoursin' on the weather, an' he talked it out about proper. He'd say, 'Wet year! Wet year!' jest like that! He got the 'wet' jest as good as I can, an', if he drawed the 'ye-ar' out a little, still any blockhead could a-told what he was sayin', an' in a voice pretty an' clear as a bell. Then he got love-sick, an' begged for comp'ny until he broke me all up. An' if I'd a-been a hen redbird I wouldn't a-been so long comin'. Had me pulverized in less'n no time! Then a little hen comes 'long, an' stops with him; an' 'twas like an organ playin' prayers to hear him tell her how he loved her. Now they've got a nest full o' the cunningest little topknot babies, an' he's splittin' the echoes, calling for the whole neighbourhood to come see 'em, he's so mortal proud.

"Stake my life he's never been fired on afore! He's pretty near wild with narvousness, but he's got too much spunk to leave his fam'ly, an' go off an' hide from creatures like you. They's no caution in him. Look at him tearin' 'round to give you another chance!

"I felt most too rheumaticky to tackle field work this spring until he come 'long, an' the fire o' his coat an' song got me warmed up as I ain't been in years. Work's gone like it was greased, an' my soul's been singin' for joy o' life an' happiness ev'ry minute o' the time since he come. Been carryin' him grub to that top rail once an' twice a day for the last month, an' I can go in three feet o' him. My wife comes to see him, an' brings him stuff; an' we about worship him. Who are you, to come 'long an' wipe out his joy in life, an' our joy in him, for jest nothin'? You'd a left him to rot on the ground, if you'd a hit him; an' me an' Maria's loved him so!

"D'you ever stop to think how full this world is o' things to love, if your heart's jest big enough to let 'em in? We love to live for the beauty o' the things surroundin' us, an' the joy we take in bein' among 'em. An' it's my belief 'at the way to make folks love us, is for us to be able to 'preciate what they can do. If a man's puttin' his heart an' soul, an' blood, an' beef-steak, an' bones into paintin' picters, you can talk farmin' to him all day, an' he's dumb; but jest show him 'at you see what he's a-drivin' at in his work, an' he'll love you like a brother. Whatever anybody succeeds in, it's success 'cos they so love it 'at they put the best o' theirselves into it; an' so, lovin' what they do, is lovin' them.

"It 'ud 'bout kill a painter-man to put the best o' himself into his picture, an' then have some fellow like you come 'long an' pour turpentine on it jest to see the paint run; an' I think it must pretty well use God up, to figure out how to make an' colour a thing like that bird, an' then have you walk up an' shoot the little red heart out of it, jest to prove 'at you can! He's the very life o' this river bank. I'd as soon see you dig up the underbrush, an' dry up the river, an' spoil the picture they make against the sky, as to hev' you drop the red-bird. He's the red life o' the whole thing! God must a-made him when his heart was pulsin' hot

with love an' the lust o' creatin' in-com-*par*-able
things; an' He jest saw how pretty it 'ud be to dip
his featherin' into the blood He was puttin' in his
veins.

"To my mind, ain't no better way to love an'
worship God, 'an to protect an' 'preciate these fine
gifts He's given for our joy an' use. Worshipin'
that bird's a kind o' religion with me. Getting the
beauty from the sky, an' the trees, an' the grass, an'
the water 'at God made, is nothin' but doin' Him
homage. Whole earth's a sanctuary. You can worship from sky above to grass under foot.

"Course, each man has his particular altar.
Mine's in that cabin up at the bend o' the river.
Maria lives there. God never did cleaner work, 'an
when He made Maria. Lovin' her's sacrament.
She's so clean, an' pure, an' honest, an' big-
hearted! In forty year I've never jest durst brace
right up to Maria an' try to put in words what she
means to me. Never saw nothin' else as beautiful,
or as good. No flower's as fragrant an' smelly as
her hair on her pillow. Never tapped a bee tree

with honey sweet as her lips a-twitchin' with a love quiver. Ain't a bird 'long the ol' Wabash with a voice up to hers. Love o' God ain't broader'n her kindness. When she's been home to see her folks, I've been so hungry for her 'at I've gone to her closet an' kissed the hem o' her skirts more'n once. I've never yet dared kiss her feet, but I've always wanted to. I've laid out 'at if she dies first, I'll do it then. An' Maria 'ud cry her eyes out if you'd a-hit the redbird. Your trappin's look like you could shoot. I guess 'twas God made that shot fly the mark. I guess——"

"If you can stop, for the love of mercy do it!" cried the hunter. His face was a sickly white, his temples wet with sweat, and his body trembling. "I can't endure any more. I don't suppose you think I've any human instincts at all; but I have a few, and I see the way to arouse more. You probably won't believe me, but I'll never kill another innocent harmless thing; and I will never lie again so long as I live."

He leaned his gun against the thorn tree, and

dropped the remainder of his hunter's outfit beside it on the ground.

"I don't seem a fit subject to 'have dominion,'" he said. "I'll leave those thing for you; and thank you for what you have done for me."

There was a crash through the bushes, a leap over the fence, and Abram and the Cardinal were alone.

The old man sat down suddenly on a fallen limb of the sycamore. He was almost dazed with astonishment. He held up his shaking hands, and watched them wonderingly, and then cupped one over each trembling knee to steady himself. He outlined his dry lips with the tip of his tongue, and breathed in heavy gusts. He glanced toward the thorn tree.

"Left his gun," he hoarsely whispered, "an' it's fine as a fiddle. Lock, stock, an' barrel just a-shinin'. An' all that heap o' leather fixin's. Must a-cost a lot o' money. Said he wasn't fit to use 'em! Lept the fence like a panther, an' cut dirt across the corn field. An' left me the gun! Well! Well!

Well! Wonder what I said? I must a-been almost *fierce*."

"See here! See here!" shrilled the Cardinal.

Abram looked him over carefully. He was quivering with fear, but in no way injured.

"My! but that was a close call, ol' fellow," said Abram. "Minute later, an' our fun 'ud a-been over, an' the summer jest spoiled. Wonder if you knew what it meant, an' if you'll be gun-shy after this. Land knows, I hope so; for a few more such doses 'ull jest lay me up."

He gathered himself together at last, set the gun over the fence, and climbing after it, caught Nancy, who had feasted to plethora on young corn. He fastened up the trace-chains, and climbing to her back, laid the gun across his lap and rode to the barn. He attended the mare with particular solicitude, and bathed his face and hands in the water trough to make himself a little more presentable to Maria. He started to the house, but had only gone a short way when he stopped, and after standing in thought for a time, turned back to the barn and gave Nancy another ear of corn.

"After all, it was all you, ol' girl," he said, patting her shoulder, "I never on earth could a-made it on time afoot."

He was so tired he leaned for support against her, for the unusual exertion and intense excitement were telling on him sorely, and as he rested he confided to her: "I don't know as I ever in my life was so riled, Nancy. I'm afraid I was a little mite fierce."

He exhibited the gun, and told the story very soberly at supper time; and Maria was so filled with solicitude for him and the bird, and so indignant at the act of the hunter, that she never said a word about Abram's torn clothing and the hours of patching that would ensue. She sat looking at the gun and thinking intently for a long time; and then she said pityingly:

"I don't know jest what you could a-said 'at 'ud make a man go off an' leave a gun like that. Poor fellow! I do hope, Abram, you didn't come down on him too awful strong. Maybe he lost his mother

144

when he was jest a little tyke, an' he hasn't had much teachin'."

Abram was completely worn out, and went early to bed. Far in the night Maria felt him fumbling around her face in an effort to learn if she were covered; and as he drew the sheet over her shoulder he muttered in worn and sleepy tones: "I'm afraid they's no use denyin' it, Maria, *I was jest mortal fierce.*"

In the sumac the frightened little mother cardinal was pressing her precious babies close against her breast; and all through the night she kept calling to her mate, "Chook! Chook!" and was satisfied only when an answering "Chip!" came. As for the Cardinal, he had learned a new lesson. He had not been under fire before. Never again would he trust any one carrying a shining thing that belched fire and smoke. He had seen the hunter coming, and had raced home to defend his mate and babies, thus making a brilliant mark of himself; and as he would not have deserted them, only the arrival of the farmer had averted a

tragedy in the sumac. He did not learn to use caution for himself; but after that, if a gun came
down the shining river, he sent a warning "Chip!"
to his mate, telling her to crouch low in her nest
and keep very quiet, and then, in broken waves of
flight, and with chirp and flutter, he exposed himself until he had lured danger from his beloved
ones.

When the babies grew large enough for their
mother to leave them a short time, she assisted in
food hunting, and the Cardinal was not so busy.
He then could find time frequently to mount to
the top of the dogwood, and cry to the world, "See
here! See here!" for the cardinal babies were
splendid. But his music was broken intermittent
vocalizing now, often uttered past a beakful of
food, and interspersed with spasmodic "chips" if
danger threatened his mate and nestlings.

Despite all their care, it was not so very long
until trouble came to the sumac; and it was all
because the first-born was plainly greedy; much
more so than either his little brother or his sister,

and he was one day ahead of them in strength. He always pushed himself forward, cried the loudest and longest, and so took the greater part of the food carried to the nest; and one day, while he was still quite awkward and uncertain, he climbed to the edge and reached so far that he fell. He rolled down the river bank, splash! into the water; and a hungry old pickerel, sunning in the weeds, finished him at a snap. He made a morsel so fat, sweet, and juicy that the pickerel lingered close for a week, waiting to see if there would be any more accidents.

The Cardinal, hunting grubs in the corn field, heard the frightened cries of his mate, and dashed to the sumac in time to see the poor little ball of brightly tinted feathers disappear in the water and to hear the splash of the fish. He called in helpless panic and fluttered over the spot. He watched and waited until there was no hope of the nestling coming up, then he went to the sumac to try to comfort his mate. She could not be convinced that her young one was gone, and for the remainder of the day filled the air with alarm cries and notes of wailing.

The two that remained were surely the envy of Birdland. The male baby was a perfect copy of his big crimson father, only his little coat was gray; but it was so highly tinged with red that it was brilliant, and his beak and feet were really red; and how his crest did flare, and how proud and important he felt, when he found he could raise and lower it at will. His sister was not nearly so bright as he, and she was almost as greedy as the lost brother. With his father's chivalry he allowed her to crowd in and take the most of the seeds and berries, so that she continually appeared as if she could swallow no more, yet she was constantly calling for food.

She took the first flight, being so greedy she forgot to be afraid, and actually flew to a neighbouring thorn tree to meet the Cardinal, coming with food, before she realized what she had done. For once gluttony had its proper reward. She not only missed the bite, but she got her little self mightily

148

well scared. With popping eyes and fear-flattened crest, she clung to the thorn limb, shivering at the depths below; and it was the greatest comfort when her brother plucked up courage and came sailing across to her. But, of course, she could not be expected to admit that. When she saw how easily he did it, she flared her crest, turned her head indifferently, and inquired if he did not find flying a very easy matter, once he mustered courage to try it; and she made him very much ashamed indeed because he had allowed her to be the first to leave the nest. From the thorn tree they worked their way to the dead sycamore; but there the lack of foliage made them so conspicuous that their mother almost went into spasms from fright, and she literally drove them back to the sumac.

The Cardinal was so inordinately proud, and made such a brave showing of teaching them to fly, bathe, and all the other things necessary for young birds to know, that it was a great mercy they escaped with their lives. He had mastered many lessons, but he never could be taught how to be quiet and conceal himself. With explosive "chips" flaming and flashing, he met dangers that sent all the other birds beside the shining river racing to cover. Concealment he scorned; and repose he never knew.

It was a summer full of rich experience for the Cardinal. After these first babies were raised and had flown, two more nests were built, and two other broods flew around the sumac. By fall the Cardinal was the father of a small flock, and they were each one neat, trim, beautiful river birds.

He had lived through spring with its perfumed air, pale flowers, and burning heart hunger. He had known summer in its golden mood, with forests pungent with spicebush and sassafras; festooned with wild grape, woodbine, and bittersweet; carpeted with velvet moss and starry mandrake peeping from beneath green shades; the never-ending murmur of the shining river; and the rich fulfilment of love's fruition.

Now it was fall, and all the promises of spring were accomplished. The woods were glorious in autumnal tints. There were ripened red haws, black haws, and wild grapes only waiting for severe frosts, nuts rattling down, scurrying squirrels, and the rabbits' flash of gray and brown. The waysides were bright with the glory of goldenrod, and royal with the purple of asters and ironwort. There was the rustle of falling leaves, the flitting of velvety butterflies, the whir of wings trained southward, and the call of the king crow gathering his followers.

Then to the Cardinal came the intuition that it was time to lead his family to the orange orchard. One day they flamed and rioted up and down the shining river, raced over the corn field, and tilted on the sumac. The next, a black frost had stripped its antlered limbs. Stark and deserted it stood, a picture of loneliness.

O bird of wonderful plumage and human-like song! What a precious thought of Divinity to create such beauty and music for our pleasure! Brave songster of the flaming coat, too proud to hide your flashing beauty, too fearless to be causious of the many dangers that beset you, from the top of the morning we greet you, and hail you King of Birdland, at your imperious command: "See here! See here!"